Hardly ... thought ... to a halt at the lodge front door.

And yet it had been wonderful. She had been with the professor for hours, and even if she hadn't been sure before, she knew now that there wasn't another man like him—not for her, anyway.

He came around the hood of the car, opened Eliza's door and lifted her out to place her gently on the porch.

"Go down to the cottage through the house," he advised her. "I'll bring the parcels."

She did as she was told, and found the little place warm and lighted, and a tea tray laid ready. Eliza would put the kettle on and when Christian came they would have a cup of tea. But when the professor did come, five minutes later, he gave her a bleak refusal when she suggested it. At the door he halted, though, when Eliza said in a level little voice, "Thank you for my lunch and for driving me, Professor. It was a lovely day."

He turned right round and looked at her frowningly. He said almost angrily, "A lovely day." And then, as though the words were being dragged out of him, "And a lovely girl."

Romance readers around the world were sad to note the passing of **Betty Neels** in June 2001. Her career spanned thirty years, and she continued to write into her ninetieth year. To her millions of fans, Betty epitomized the romance writer, and yet she began writing almost by accident. She had retired from nursing, but her inquiring mind still sought stimulation. Her new career was born when she heard a lady in her local library bemoaning the lack of good romance novels. Betty's first book, *Sister Peters in Amsterdam,* was published in 1969, and she eventually completed 134 books. Her novels offer a reassuring warmth that was very much a part of her own personality. She was a wonderful writer, and she will be greatly missed. Her spirit and genuine talent will live on in all her stories.

THE BEST *of*

BETTY NEELS

HEAVEN IS GENTLE

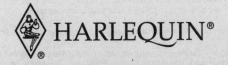

HARLEQUIN®

TORONTO • NEW YORK • LONDON
AMSTERDAM • PARIS • SYDNEY • HAMBURG
STOCKHOLM • ATHENS • TOKYO • MILAN • MADRID
PRAGUE • WARSAW • BUDAPEST • AUCKLAND

ISBN-13: 978-0-373-19900-6
ISBN-10:   0-373-19900-7

HEAVEN IS GENTLE

CHAPTER ONE

THE room was large and well lighted, and by reason of the cheerful fire in the wide chimneypiece and the thick curtains drawn against the grey January afternoon, cosy enough. There were three persons in it; an elderly man, sitting at his ease behind a very large, extremely untidy desk, a thin, prim woman at a small table close by and a tall, broad-shouldered man sitting astride a small chair, his arms folded across its back, his square, determined chin resting on two large and well cared for hands. He was a handsome man, his dark hair silvered at the temples, and possessing a pair of formidable black brows above very dark eyes. In repose he appeared to be of an age approaching forty, but when he smiled, and he was smiling now, he looked a good deal younger.

Miss Trim paused in the reading of the names from a typed list before her and glanced at the two men. They were smoking pipes and she gave a small protesting cough which she knew would be ignored, anyhow.

'They sound like a line of chorus girls,' commented the younger of her two companions. His smile turned to an engaging grin. 'How do you like the idea of being nursed by a Shirley Anne, or an Angela, or—what was that last one, Miss Trim? A Felicity?'

His elderly companion puffed a smoke ring and viewed it with satisfaction. 'We should have tried for a male nurse,' he mused out loud, 'but from a psychological point of view that would not have been satisfactory.'

'There are still a few names on the list, Professor Wyllie.' Miss Trim sounded faintly tart, probably because of the smoke wreathing itself around her head. She coughed again and continued to read: 'Annette Dawes, Marilyn Jones, Eliza Proudfoot, Heather Cox…'

She was interrupted. 'A moment, Miss Trim—that name again, Eliza…?'

'Miss Eliza Proudfoot, Professor van Duyl.'

'This is the one,' his deep voice with its faint trace of an accent, sounded incisive. 'With a name like that, I don't see how we can go wrong.'

He glanced at the older man, his eyebrows lifted. 'What do you say, sir?'

'You're probably right. Let's hear the details, Miss Trim.'

Before she could speak: 'Five foot ten,' murmured Professor van Duyl, 'with vital statistics to match.' He caught the secretary's disapproving eye. 'She'll need to be strong,' he reminded her blandly, 'not young any

more, rather on the plain side and decidedly motherly.'
He turned his smiling gaze on Professor Wyllie. 'Will
you like that?'

His companion chuckled. 'I daresay she will do as
well as any, provided that her qualifications are good.'
He gave Miss Trim a questioning look, and she
answered promptly, mentioning one of the larger
London hospitals.

'She trained there,' she recited from her meticulous
notes, 'and is now Ward Sister of Men's Medical. She
is twenty-eight years old, unmarried, and thought very
highly of by those members of the medical profession
for whom she works.' She added primly, 'Shall I telephone Sir Harry Bliss, Professor? He is the consultant
in charge of her ward.'

'Good lord, woman,' exploded her employer, 'you
don't have to tell me that! Of course I know it's old
Harry—known him man and boy, whatever that's
supposed to mean. Get him on the telephone and then
go away and concoct the right sort of letter to send to
this young woman.'

'You wish to interview her, sir?'

'No, no. There's no time for that; if Harry says she's
OK she'll do. We go to Inverpolly on the tenth; ask her
to come up there whichever way she likes to by the fifteenth—expenses paid, of course. See that she gets a
good idea how to reach the place and add a few trim-
mings—benefit to mankind and all that stuff. Oh, and

warn her that she must be prepared to look after me as well if I should have an attack.'

He waved a hand at Miss Trim and she understood herself to be dismissed as she murmured suitably, thanked Professor van Duyl for opening the door for her and went back to her own office, where she set about composing a suitable letter to Miss Proudfoot, thinking as she did so that the young lady in question would need to be tough indeed if she accepted the post she was couching in such cautiously attractive terms. Conditions in the Highlands of Wester Ross at this time of year would be hard enough, working for the two men she had just left harder still. Professor Wyllie was a dear old man, but after acting as his secretary for fifteen years, she knew him inside out; he was irascible at times, wildly unpredictable, and his language when he was in a bad temper was quite unprintable. And as for Professor van Duyl—Miss Trim paused in her typing and her rather sharp features relaxed into a smile. She had met him on several occasions over the last five years or so, and while he had been unfailingly courteous and charming towards her, she sensed that here was a man with a nasty temper, nicely under control, and a very strong will behind that handsome face. As she finished her letter, she found herself hoping that Miss Proudfoot was good at managing men as well as being tough.

The subject of her thoughts, blithely unaware of the future hurtling towards her, was doing a round with Sir

Harry Bliss, his registrar—one Donald Jones, a clutch of worried housemen, and the social worker, a beaky-nosed lady with a heart of gold, known throughout the hospital as Ducky. And keeping an eye on the whole bunch of them was Staff Nurse Mary Price, an amiable beanpole of a girl, much prized by Sister Proudfoot, and her willing slave as well as friend. She sidled up to her now, bent down and whispered urgently, listened in her turn, nodded and sped away.

'And where is our little Mary Price going?' enquired Sir Harry without lifting his eyes from the notes he was reading. There was a faint murmur of laughter because he prided himself on his sense of humour, but Sister Proudfoot who had heard that one a dozen times before merely handed him the patient's chart as the housemen fanned out into a respectful semi-circle around the foot of the bed. 'It's time for nurses' dinner,' she said in a composed voice.

'Implying that I am too slow on my round, Sister?' He stared down at her over his glasses.

She gave him a serene glance. 'No, sir—just stating a fact.' She smiled at him and he rumbled out a laugh. 'All right, all right—let's get on with the job, then. Let me see Mr Atkins' chest.'

She bent to the patient, a small, shapely girl with bright golden hair swept into a neat bun from which little curls escaped. Her eyes were unexpectedly hazel, richly fringed, her nose small and straight and her mouth sweetly curved. A very pretty girl, who looked years younger than her age and far too fragile for her job.

She was on her way back from a late dinner when the faithful Staff came hurrying to meet her. 'They've just telephoned from the office—Miss Smythe wants to see you at once, Sister.' She beamed down at Eliza like a good-natured stork. 'I'll start the medicines, shall I, and get old Mr Pearce ready for X-ray.'

Eliza nodded. 'Yes, do. I wonder what I've done,' she mused. 'Do you suppose it's because I complained about the shortage of linen bags? You know we have to be careful nowadays.' She added a little vaguely, 'Unions and things.'

'But you weren't nasty,' Mary reassured her, 'you never are.'

Eliza beamed at her. 'What a great comfort you always are, Mary. We'll have a cup of tea when I get back and I'll tell you all about it.'

She turned round and sped back the way she had come, up and down corridors and a staircase or so, until she came to the Office door, where she stopped for a moment to fetch her breath before tapping on it, and in response to the green light above it, entered.

Miss Smythe, the Principal Nursing Officer, was sitting at her desk. She was a stern-faced woman, but at the moment Eliza was relieved to see that she was looking quite amiable. She waved a hand at a chair, said, 'Good afternoon, Sister Proudfoot,' waited until

Eliza had sat down and began: 'I have received a letter about you, and with it a letter for yourself—from Professor Wyllie.'

Wyllie, thought Eliza, a shade uneasily, the name rang a bell; asthma research and heart complications or something of that sort, and hadn't someone told her once that he himself was a sufferer? She said cautiously:

'Yes, Miss Smythe?'

For answer her superior handed her a letter. 'I suggest that you read this for yourself, Sister, and then let me have your comments.'

Miss Trim had done her work well; the letter, while astonishing Eliza very much, could not help but flatter her. She read it to its end and then looked across at Miss Smythe. 'Well, I never!' she declared.

The lady's features relaxed into the beginnings of a smile. 'I was surprised too, Sister. It is of course a great honour, which will reflect upon St Anne's. I hope that you will consider it well and agree to go.'

'It's a long way away.'

Miss Smythe's voice was smoothly persuasive. 'Yes, but I believe that you have a car? There is no reason why you shouldn't drive yourself up there, and Professor Wyllie assures me that the whole experiment, while most important to him, will take only a few weeks. Sir Harry Bliss thinks that you should avail yourself of the opportunity, it may be of the utmost advantage to you in your career.'

Eliza frowned faintly. She had never wanted a career; somehow or other it had been thrust upon her; she had enjoyed training as a nurse, she had liked staffing afterwards and when she had been offered a Sister's post she had accepted it with pleasure, never imagining that she would still be in it five years later. She wasn't a career girl at all; she had grown up with the idea of marrying and having children of her own, but despite numerous opportunities to do this, she had always hung back at the last minute, aware, somewhere at the back of her mind, that this wasn't the right man. And now here she was, as near as not twenty-nine and Miss Smythe talking as though she was going to be a Ward Sister for ever. She sighed. 'May I have a little time to think about it? I should like to see exactly where this place is and discover precisely what it's all about. Am I to be the only woman there?'

'Yes, so I understand. That is why they wanted a somewhat older girl, and a trained nurse, of course. As a precaution, I believe; Professor Wyllie is a sufferer from asthma as well as having heart failure; his health must be safe-guarded. Over and above that, he seems to think that a woman nurse would be of more benefit to the patients. There will also be a number of technicians, the patients, of course—and a colleague of the professor's. A Dutch Professor of Medicine, highly thought of, I believe.'

Eliza dismissed him at once; he would be learned and

bald and use long words in a thick accent, like the elderly brilliant friend of Sir Harry Bliss, who had discussed each patient at such length that she had had to go without her dinner.

'Let me know by this evening, Sister Proudfoot,' advised Miss Smythe, 'sooner if you can manage it— it seems that Professor Wyllie wants an answer as soon as possible.'

An observation which almost decided Eliza to refuse out of sheer perversity; she was by nature an obliging girl, but she didn't like being pushed; there were several things she wanted to know about the job, and no chance of finding out about any of them in such a short time. She walked back through the hospital, her head bowed in thought, so that when she narrowly avoided bumping into Sir Harry she was forced to stop and apologise.

'Deep in thought,' pronounced that gentleman, 'about that job my old friend Willy Wyllie has offered you, eh? Oh, I thought so—take it, girl, it will make a nice change from this place, put a bit of colour into those cheeks and a pound or two on to your bones.'

Eliza stared at him thoughtfully. 'Probably,' she agreed amiably. 'You seem to know all about it, sir, but I don't, do I? I mean the bare facts are in the letter, but where do I live while I'm there, and what about time off and how far away is it from the shops and shall I be expected to do night duty?'

'Tell you what,' said Sir Harry, 'we'll go and tele-phone someone this very minute and find out.'

'But I'm on duty. And you, sir, if I might remind you, are expected in Women's Medical…' She glanced at her watch. 'You were expected…' she corrected herself demurely, 'fifteen minutes ago.'

'In that case, five minutes more won't be noticed.' He swept her along with him to the consultants' room, opened the door and thrust her inside ahead of him. 'Well, really,' began Eliza, and seeing it was hopeless to say anything, watched him pick up the telephone and demand a number.

He talked for some minutes, firing questions at his unseen listener like bullets from a gun, and presently said: 'Hold on, I'll ask her.'

'Two days off a week, but probably you won't get them, three hours off a day, these to be arranged accord-ing to the day's requirements. You will have a little cottage to live in—by yourself, close to the main house. There will be an opportunity to go to the nearest town and shop if you should wish to, but it's only fair to mention that there isn't much in the way of entertainment.' He barely gave her time to absorb this sparse information before he barked: 'Well, how about it, Eliza?' He grinned at her. 'I recommended you, you can't let me down.'

She gave him a severe look. 'Did you now, sir? Miss Smythe said that I could think it over.'

'That was before you knew all these details I've gone

to so much trouble to discover for you,' he wheedled. 'Come on now—it'll make a nice change.'

She gave him a sudden smile. 'All right, though I shall have to miss the hospital ball.'

He had picked up the receiver again. 'Pooh, you can go dancing any night of the week; there isn't a man in the hospital who hasn't asked you out, one way and another.' He turned away before she could reply and spoke to the patient soul at the other end of the line. 'OK, she'll come. Details later.' And when she started to protest at his high-handed methods: 'Well, why not, girl? You said you would go—you can fix the details with Miss Smythe.' He bustled her to the door. 'And now I'm late for my round, and it's your fault.'

He trod on his way, leaving her speechless with indignation.

Mary Price had tea ready, the ward under control and five minutes to spare when Eliza got back to Men's Medical. They sipped the dark, sweet brew in the peace and quiet of the office while Eliza explained briefly about the strange offer she had been made.

'Oh, take it, Sister,' begged her faithful colleague. 'We shall miss you dreadfully, but it'll only be for a week or two, and think of the fun you'll have.' Her brown eyes sparkled at the thought. 'You could go up by car.'

'Um,' said Eliza, 'so I could. Miss Smythe said that I'd been chosen from quite a long list of likely nurses. Why me, I wonder?'

'Sir Harry, of course—you said yourself that he knew all about it.' She refilled their cups. 'What are you supposed to do once you're there?'

'I'm not quite sure. It's an experiment—cardiac asthma as well as the intrinsic and extrinsic kinds—they want to prove something or other about climate and the effect of complete freedom from stress or strain.'

'Sounds interesting. When do you have to leave?'

'I have to report for duty on the fifteenth,' she peered at the calendar, 'eight days' time. We'll have to do something about the off duty, if you have a weekend before I go…'

They became immersed in the complicated jigsaw of days off, and presently, having got everything arranged to their mutual satisfaction, they left the office; Staff to supervise the return of the convalescent patients to their beds and Sister Proudfoot to cast her professional eye over the ward in general.

So that Mary might get her weekend off before she herself went away, Eliza took her own days off a couple of days later. She left the hospital after a long day's work, driving her Fiat 500, a vehicle she had acquired some five years previously and saw little hope of replacing for the next few years at least. But even though it was by now a little shabby, and the engine made strange noises from time to time, it still served her well. She turned its small nose towards the west now, and after what seemed an age of slow driving through London, reached its outskirts and at length the M3. Here at least she could travel as fast as the Fiat would allow, and even when the motorway gave way to the Winchester bypass, she maintained a steady fifty miles an hour, only once past Winchester and on the Romsey road, she slowed down a little. It was very dark, and she had wasted a long time getting out of London; she wouldn't reach Charmouth until midnight. The thought of the pleasant house where her parents lived spurred her on; they would wait up for her, they always did, and there would be hot soup and sausage rolls, warm and featherlight from the oven. Eliza, who hadn't stopped for supper, put her small foot down on the accelerator.

The road was dark and lonely once she had passed Cadnam Corner. She left the New Forest behind, skirted Ringwood and threaded her way through Wimborne, silent under the blanket of winter clouds. Dorchester was silent too—she was getting near home now, there were only the hills between her and Bridport and then down and up through Chideock and then home. Here eager thoughts ran ahead of her, so that it seemed nearer than it actually was.

The lights of the house were still on as she brought the little car to a halt at the top of the hill at the further end of the little town, it lay back from the road, flanked by neighbours, all three of them little Regency houses, bowfronted, with verandahs and roomy front gardens. She was out of the car, her case in her hand, and running up the garden path almost as soon as she had switched off the engine; the cold bit into her as she turned the old-fashioned brass knob of the door and went inside. Her mother and father were still up, as she knew they would be, sitting one each side of the open fire, dozing a little, to wake as she went into the room. She embraced them with affection; her mother, as small a woman as she was, her father, tall and thin and scholarly. 'Darlings,' she declared, 'how lovely to see you! It seems ages since I was home and I've heaps to tell you. I'll just run the car across the road.'

She flew outside again; the car park belonged to the hotel opposite but the manager never minded her using it. She tucked the Fiat away in a corner and went back indoors, to find the soup and the sausage rolls, just as she had anticipated, waiting for her. She gobbled delicately and between mouthfuls began to tell her parents about the unexpected job she had been asked to take. 'There was a list,' she explained. 'Heaven knows how they made it in the first place or why they picked on me—with a pin, most likely. I almost decided not to accept it, but Sir Harry Bliss thought it would be a good idea—and it's only for a few weeks.'

Her mother offered her another sausage roll. 'Yes, darling, I see. But isn't this place miles away from everywhere?'

'Yes. But I'm to have my own cottage to live in and

I daresay I'll be too busy to want to do much when I'm not on duty.'

'There will be another nurse there?' asked her father.

She shook her head. 'No—I'm the only one and it sounds as though I shan't have much to do. A handful of volunteer patients—all men, a few technicians and the two professors; William Wyllie—he's an asthma case himself and I may have to look after him; he's quite old—well, not very old, touching seventy.'

'And the other doctor?' It was her mother this time.

'Oh, a friend of his. I daresay he'll have asthma too, he'll certainly be elderly.' She brushed the crumbs from her pretty mouth and sat back with a sigh of content. 'Now tell me all the news, my dears. Have you heard from Henry? and has Pat got over the measles?'

Henry was a younger brother, working in Brussels for the Common Market, and Pat was her small niece, her younger sister Polly's daughter, who had married several years earlier. Her mother embarked on family news, wondering as she did so why it was that this pretty little creature sitting beside her hadn't married herself, years ago. Of course she didn't look anything like her age, but thirty wasn't far off; Mrs Proudfoot belonged to the generation which considered thirty to be getting a little long in the tooth, and she worried about Eliza. The dear girl had had her chances—was still having them; she knew for a fact that at least two eligible young men had proposed to her during the last six months. And now she was off to this godforsaken spot in the Highlands where, as far as she could make out, there wasn't going to be a man under sixty.

The two days passed quickly; there was so much to do, so many friends to visit, as well as helping her mother in the nice old house and going for walks with her father, who, now that he had retired from the Civil Service, found time to indulge in his hobby of fossil gathering. Eliza, who knew nothing about fossils, obligingly accompanied him to the beach and collected what she hoped were fine specimens, and which were almost always just pebbles. All the same, they enjoyed each other's company and the fresh air gave her a glow which made her prettier than ever, so that one of the eligible young men, meeting her by chance in the main street, took the instant opportunity of proposing for a second time, an offer which she gently refused, aware that she was throwing away a good chance.

She worried about it as she drove herself back to London. Charlie King was an old friend, she had known him for years; he would make a splendid husband and he had a good job. She would, she decided, think about him seriously while she was away in Scotland; no doubt there would be time to think while she was there, and being a long way from a problem often caused it to appear in a quite different light. She put the thought away firmly for the time being and concentrated on her driving, for there had been a frost overnight, and the road was treacherous.

The next few days went rapidly, for she was busy. Mary Price had gone on her promised weekend the day after she got back and although she had two part-time staff nurses to help her, there was a good deal of extra paper work because she was going away. It was nice to see Mary back again and talk over the managing of the ward while she was away. Eliza spent her last day smoothing out all the last-minute problems, bade her patients and staff a temporary goodbye and went off duty to while away an hour with her friends in the Sisters' sitting room before going to her room to pack ready for an early start in the morning—warm clothes and not too many of them—thick sweaters and slacks, an old anorak she had brought from home and as a special concession to the faint hope of a social life, a long mohair skirt and cashmere top in a pleasing shade of old rose.

She left really early the following morning, her friends' good wishes ringing in her ears, instructions as to how to reach her destination written neatly on the pad beside the map on the seat beside her. She planned to take two, perhaps three days to get to Inverpolly, for although the Fiat always did its best, it wasn't capable of sustained speed; besides, the weather, cold and blustery now, might worsen and hold her up. She had three clear days in hand and she didn't suppose anyone would mind if she arrived a little sooner than that.

She made good progress. She had intended to spend

the night at York, but she found that she had several
hours in hand when she reached that city. She had an
early tea and pressed on to Darlington and then turned
on to the Penrith road where she decided to spend the
night at the George. She was well ahead of her schedule
and she felt rather pleased with herself, everything had
been much easier than she had expected. She ate a good
supper and went early to bed.

It was raining when she left, quite early, the next
morning. By the time she had got to Carlisle, it was a
steady downpour and from the look of the sky, was
likely to continue so for hours, but it was a bare two
hundred miles to Fort William, though there were
another hundred and sixty miles after that, probably
more, it was so difficult to tell from the map, but she felt
relaxed now, eager to keep on for as long as possible,
perhaps even complete the journey. She had thought at
first that she would take the road to Inverness, but the
map showed another, winding road round the lochs, she
had almost decided to try it when she reached Fort
William for a quick, late lunch, studying the map mean-
while. But it would have to be Inverness, she decided,
the coast road looked decidedly complicated, and there
was a ferry which might not be running at this time of
year. She would push on; it was only three o'clock and
roughly speaking, only another hundred and thirty miles
to go. Even allowing for the early dark, she had two
hours of driving and she was used to driving at night.

She took another look at the map and saw that she didn't need to go to Inverness at all; there was a side road which would bring her out on the road to Bonar Bridge.

It was dark when she got there and she wanted her tea, but she was too near the end of her journey to spare the time now; only another thirty miles or so to go. But she hadn't gone half that distance before she regretted her wild enthusiasm; it was a lonely road she was travelling along now and after a little while there were no villages at all and almost no traffic. To try to find the remote lodge where Professor Wyllie was working would be madness; fortunately she remembered that there was a village with an impossible name just outside the National Park of Inverpolly, she could spend the night there. She reflected rather crossly now because she was tired and thirsty and just the smallest bit nervous that it was an impossible place to reach, and if she hadn't had a car what would they have done about getting her there? Being learned men, wrapped up in their work, they had probably not given it a thought. The road appeared to be going nowhere in particular. Perhaps she was lost, and that was her own fault, of course; she should have realised that parts of the Scottish Highlands really were remote from the rest of the world. Eliza glanced at the speedometer; she had come quite a distance and passed nothing at all; she must be on the wrong road and told herself not to be a fool, for there had been no other road to take. It was then she saw the signpost. Inchnadamph, one mile.

The hotel was pleasant; warm and friendly too, although by now she was so tired that a barn would have been heaven. They gave her a large, old-fashioned room and fed her like a queen because there was only a handful of guests and they had already dined. She met them briefly when she went to have her coffee in the lounge, and then, hardly able to keep her eyes open, retired to her comfortable bed. A good sleep, she promised herself, and after breakfast she would drive the last few miles of her journey.

It was raining when she started off again, but she wasn't tired any more and she had had an enormous breakfast; even the friendly warning that the road, once she was through Lochinver, was narrow and not very good couldn't damp her good spirits; it was daylight now and she had hours of time in which to find the lodge.

They were right about the road, she discovered that quickly enough, although she found the village of Inverkirkaig easily enough. The lodge was a couple of miles further on, said her instructions; there was a track on the left of the road which would lead her to the house. But the instructions hadn't mentioned the winding, muddy road though, going steadily and steeply uphill until she began to wonder if the Fiat would make it. But she reached the track at last and turned carefully into it. It was, in fact, nothing more than a way beaten by car wheels through rough ground; the little car bounced and squelched from one pothole to the next, while the trees on either side dripped mournfully on to it. The rain had increased its intensity too. Eliza could barely see before her, but when at last she turned a corner, she saw the lodge in front of her, a depressing enough sight in the rain, and as far as she could see as she drew up before its shabby door, badly in need of a paint. She got out and banged the iron knocker; the place was a disgrace. Possibly the two professors, blind to everything but their work, had noticed nothing. That was the worst of elderly gentlemen with single-track minds. There was a movement behind the door. She edged a little nearer out of the rain and waited for it to be opened.

CHAPTER TWO

SHE had expected someone—a woman from the village she had just passed through, perhaps—as faded and neglected as the house to open the door, not this enormous, elegant man with his dark crusader's face, dressed, her quick eye noted, with all the care of a man about to stroll down St James' to his club, instead of roughing it in this back-of-beyond spot. The owner of the place? A visitor?

She became aware that the rain was trickling down the back of her neck and she frowned. 'I'm the nurse,' she stated baldly, since it seemed there were no niceties of introduction. 'Perhaps you'll be kind enough to let Professor Wyllie know that I'm here.'

The tall man made no move, indeed he blocked the whole of the doorway with his bulk; for one awful moment Eliza wondered if she had come to the wrong place and added anxiously: 'Professor Wyllie is here, isn't he?'

He nodded, and now she could see that his dark eyes were gleaming with laughter. 'Miss Eliza Proudfoot,' he said slowly, not addressing her really; merely confirming his own thoughts. 'Five foot ten and buxom…'

She stared at him in amazement. 'I beg your pardon?' Her voice was acid—forgivable enough; she wanted to get in out of the rain and a cup of coffee would be welcome. She added crossly: 'I'm getting wet.'

She was plucked inside as though she had been a wet kitten. 'Forgive me.' His voice was politely concerned, but she could sense his amusement too. 'Is that your car?'

'Yes.'

He stared down at her. 'Such a pretty girl, and such a pretty voice too, though decidedly acidulated at the moment.'

He paid her the compliment and took it away again with a lazy charm which infuriated her. 'Are you the owner of this place?' she wanted to know.

He looked faintly surprised. 'As a matter of fact, I am.'

'Then perhaps you will tell me where I can find Professor Wyllie, since you seem unwilling to take me to him.' She added nastily: 'My case is in the car.'

He chuckled at that and opened the door again, so that she immediately felt forced to exclaim: 'You can't go out like that—you'll ruin that good suit!'

He looked down at his large person. 'The only one I have,' he murmured apologetically.

'Well, then…Professor Wyllie?'

He turned without a word and led her down the hall,

past a rather nice staircase which needed a good dust, and opened a door. The room was a study, overflowing with books and papers, and sitting in the middle of it all was an elderly gentleman, who looked up as they went in, peering at them over his half glasses with guileless blue eyes.

'Miss Eliza Proudfoot,' announced the large man blandly, and now there was no hiding the amusement in his voice.

'God bless my soul!' exclaimed Mr Wyllie, and took off his glasses and polished them.

Eliza took a few steps towards the desk at which he sat. She was fast coming to the conclusion that either she was dealing with eccentrics, or the whole affair was some colossal mistake. But she had been dealing with men of every age and sort, and ill at that, for a number of years now; she said in a matter-of-fact voice: 'You weren't expecting me.'

She had addressed the older man, but it was the man who had admitted her who answered. 'Oh, indeed we were, although I must admit at the same time that we weren't expecting—er—quite you.'

She gave him a cool look, she wasn't sure that she liked him. 'That's no answer,' she pointed out, and then suddenly seeing his point, cried out: 'Oh, I'm the wrong nurse, is that it? Five foot ten and buxom…but I really am Eliza Proudfoot.'

'What was old Harry about?' demanded Professor Wyllie of no one in particular. 'Why, you're far too small to be of any use, and no one will make me believe that you're almost twenty-nine.'

She winced; no girl likes to have her age bandied about once she is over twenty-one. 'I'm very strong, and I've been in charge of Men's Medical at St Anne's for more than five years, and if you are acquainted with Sir Harry Bliss you'll know that if he said I could do the job, then there's no more to be said.'

'We don't know about being motherly yet, but she's tough,' remarked the large man. He was sitting on the edge of the desk, one well-shod, enormous foot swinging gently.

She shot him an annoyed glance and walked deliberately across the room to stand before him. It was a little disconcerting when he rose politely to his feet, so that she was forced to crane her neck in order to see his face. 'You have done nothing but make remarks about me since you opened the door,' her voice was crisp and, she hoped, reasonable, 'and I can't think why you are trying to frighten me away—because you are, aren't you? But since you only own the house—and you should be ashamed to have let it lapse into such a neglected state,' she admonished him in passing, 'I really can't see why you should interfere with my appointment. I've come to work for Professor Wyllie, not you.'

The dark face broke into a slow smile. 'My dear young lady, I must correct you; you have come to work for me too.' He held out a hand that looked as though it

had never seen hard work in its life. 'I quite neglected
to introduce myself—Professor Christian van Duyl.'

Eliza allowed her hand to be wrung while she recovered from her surprise. She was still framing a suitable
answer to this bombshell when he gave her back her
hand and started for the door.

'I'll see about your luggage and put the car away,' he
told her, 'while you and Professor Wyllie have a chat.'
He turned to the door. 'You would like some coffee,
Miss Proudfoot?'

She nodded and then looked at the elderly gentleman
behind the desk. He was smiling, a friendly smile, she
was glad to see. 'Excuse me getting up, girl…I shall call
you Eliza if I may—which means that I grow abo-
minably lazy. You came up by car?'

She sat down in the chair he had indicated. 'Yes,' and
she couldn't refrain from asking innocently, 'How else
does one get here?'

He grinned. 'Helicopter?'

'If I had known that this place was so remote, I might
have thought of that.'

He was studying her quietly. 'It's beautiful here in the
autumn and late spring.'

'Surely the climate is all wrong for asthma cases?'

He chuckled. 'That's part of the exercise. Professor
van Duyl and I have established that the stress and strain
of modern life are just as much deciding factors in
bringing on attacks as the wrong climate—now we need

to prove that. We have ten volunteer patients with us—five Dutch, five English, and we intend to test our theory. If it holds water, then it gives us a lead, however slender, in the treatment of the wretched complaint.'

'Why did you want a nurse, sir?'

'We want the patients to feel secure—it is remark-able what a nurse's uniform will do on that score, and you will have work to do—general duties,' he looked vague—'and of course you will need to deal with any attacks which may crop up—one or two of the men are cardiac cases, but we will go into all that later. They warned you, I hope, that I'm an asthmatic myself with a touch of cardiac failure—I daresay you will be a lot busier than you think.'

He looked up as the door opened and Professor van Duyl came in, followed by a stocky, middle-aged man bearing a tray set neatly with a large coffee pot, milk, sugar and a selection of mugs. He set it down on a table which Professor van Duyl swept free of papers and books, smiled paternally at her, and disappeared discreetly. She wondered who he was, but as no one volunteered this information, she supposed him to be one of the staff, then forgot him as she poured the coffee.

She learned a good deal during the next hour; she liked Professor Wyllie, even though he did get carried away with his subject from time to time, leaving her a little out of her depth, and as for Professor van Duyl, he treated her with a tolerant amusement which annoyed her very much, while at the same time telling her all she would need to know. It was he who outlined her duties, gave her working hours and explained that the ten patients were housed very comfortably in a Nissen hut, left over from the war, and now suitably heated and furnished to supply a degree of comfort for its inmates.

'Professor Wyllie and I sleep in this house, and so do those who work with us. We are connected by telephone to both the Nissen hut and your cottage, and although we hope that this will not be necessary, we should expect you to come immediately should you be asked for, day or night.'

She nodded; it seemed fair enough. 'Is there someone on duty with the patients during the night?' she wanted to know.

'No—we believe there to be no need. They have but to telephone for help, neither will it be necessary for you to remain on duty all day; they are all of them up patients—indeed, if they were home, they would be working.' He looked at Professor Wyllie. 'Is there anything else you want to talk to Miss Proudfoot about?' he asked. 'Would it be a good idea if she were to go over to the cottage and settle in before lunch? You will need her all the afternoon, I take it—she will have to be taken through the case notes.'

Professor Wyllie nodded agreement. 'A good idea— take her over, Christian, will you? Hub knows she's here, he'll be on the lookout presumably. Sheets and

things,' he added vaguely. For a moment he looked quite
worried so that Eliza felt constrained to say in a rallying
voice: 'I shall be quite all right, sir. I'll see you later.'

She walked beside the Dutchman down the hall and
out of the door into a light drizzle of rain, casting round
in her mind for a topic of conversation to bridge the
silence between them, but she could think of nothing,
and her companion strode along, deep in his own
thoughts, so that she saw that any idea she might have
about entertaining him with small talk was quite super-
fluous. They went round the side of the house and took
a narrow muddy path which was overgrown with coarse
grass and shrubs. There was a sharp bend in it after
only a few yards, and the cottage stood before them. It
was very small; a gardener's house, or perhaps a game-
keeper, she thought, looking at its low front door and
the small square windows on either side of it.

Her companion produced a key, opened the door and
stood aside for her to enter. It gave directly on to the
sitting room, a surprisingly cheerful little apartment,
with a window at the back and three doors leading from
it. Professor van Duyl gave her no time to do more than
glance around her, however, but went past her to open
one of the doors.

'Bedroom,' he explained briefly, 'bathroom next
door, kitchen here.' He swept open the third door. 'You
will eat with us, of course, although when you have your
free days you may do as you wish. There's a sitting

room up at the house which you are welcome to use—
there's television there and books enough. Breakfast at
eight, lunch at one—we don't have tea, but Hub will fix
that for you. Supper at eight, but that will depend on
how the day has gone.' He turned to go. 'Hub will bring
your case along in a minute and light the fire for you.'
He eyed her levelly. 'And don't get the idea that this a
nice easy job—you'll not only have the patients to see
to but a good deal of paper work as well, and remember
that you will be at our beck and call whether you're off
duty or not.'

Eliza eyed him coldly in her turn. 'Charming! I'm not
quite sure what you expected, but I'm not up to your ex-
pectations, am I? Well, I didn't expect you and you're
not up to mine—I expected a nice old gentleman like
Professor Wyllie, so at least we understand each other,
don't we, Professor?' She walked towards the bedroom,
saying over her shoulder:

'I'll see you at lunch. Thank you for bringing me over.'

She didn't see the little gleam of appreciation in his
dark eyes as he went. The door shut gently behind him
and she dismissed him from her mind and began to
explore her temporary home. It was indeed very small
but extremely cosy, the furniture was simple and unclut-
tered and someone had put a bowl of hyacinths on the
little table by one of the two easy chairs. There were nice
thick curtains at the windows, she noticed with satisfaction, and a reading lamp as well as a funny old-fash-

ioned lamp hanging from the ceiling. The bedroom was nice too, even smaller than the sitting room and furnished simply with a narrow bed, a chest of drawers and a mirror, with a shelf by the bed and a stool in one corner. There was no wardrobe or cupboard, though; presumably she would have to hang everything on the hooks behind the bedroom door. The kitchen was a mere slip of a place but adequately fitted out; she wouldn't need to cook much, anyway, but it would be pleasant to make tea or coffee in the evenings before she went to bed. She was roused from her inspection by the rattle of the door knocker and when she called 'come in', the same elderly man who had brought the coffee tray came in with her case. He smiled at her, took it into the bedroom and then went to put a match to the fire laid ready in the tiny grate.

'I can do that,' exclaimed Eliza, and when he turned to shake his head at her: 'You're Hub, aren't you? Are you Mr Hub, or is that your Christian name, and are you one of the staff?'

When he answered her she could hear that he wasn't English, although he spoke fluently enough. 'Yes, I'm Hub, miss—if you will just call me that—I'm one of the staff, as you say.' He added a log to the small blaze he had started and got to his feet. 'You will find tea and sugar and some other groceries in the kitchen cupboard, miss, and if you need anything, will you ask me and I will see that you get it.'

She thanked him and he went away; he was a kind of quartermaster, she supposed, seeing to food and drink and household supplies for all of them; she couldn't imagine either of the professors bothering their clever heads about such things.

She remembered suddenly that she had promised that she would telephone her mother when she arrived; she would just have time before she went to lunch. She picked up the receiver, not quite believing that there would be anyone there to answer her, but someone did—a man's voice with a strong Cockney accent, assuring her that he would get the number she wanted right away.

Her mother had a great many questions to ask; Eliza talked until five to one, and then wasn't finished. With a promise to write that evening, she rang off, ran a comb through her hair, looked at her face in the mirror without doing anything to it because there wasn't time and went back to the house.

Lunch, she discovered to her surprise, was a formal meal, taken in a comfortably furnished room at a table laid with care with good glass and china and well laundered table linen. There was another man there, of middle height and a little stout, pleasant-faced and in his late forties, she guessed. He was introduced as John Peters, the pharmacist and a Doctor of Science, and although he greeted her pleasantly if somewhat absent-mindedly, he had little to say for himself. It was the two professors who sustained the conversation; a pleasant miscellany of this and that, gradually drawing her into the talk as they sampled the excellent saddle of lamb, followed by an apricot upside-down pudding as light as air. Eliza had a second helping and wondered who did the cooking.

They had their coffee round the table, served by Hub, and she had only just finished pouring it when Professor van Duyl remarked smoothly:

'We should warn you that we start work tomorrow and are unlikely to take our lunch in such comfortable leisure. Indeed, I doubt if we shall meet until the evening—other than at our work, of course. You see, each attack which a patient may have must be recorded, timed and treated—and there are ten patients.' He smiled at her across the wide table, his head a little on one side, for all the world, she thought indignantly, as though he were warning her that she was there strictly for work and nothing else. The indignation showed on her face, for his smile became mocking and the black eyebrows rose.

'You have had very little time to unpack,' he observed with chilling civility, 'if you like to return to the cottage and come to the office at—let me see…' he glanced at Professor Wyllie, who nodded his head, 'half past two, when you will meet the rest of the people who are here before seeing the patients. This evening we can get together over the case notes and explain exactly what has to be done. You have your uniform with you?'

She was a little surprised. 'Yes, of course.'

'Good. May I suggest that you put it on before joining us this afternoon?'

'Very wise,' muttered Professor Wyllie, and when she looked at him enquiringly, added hastily: 'Yes, well…h'm' and added for no reason at all: 'You have a raincoat with you too, I trust? The weather in these parts can be bad at this time of year.' He coughed. 'You're a very pretty girl.'

She went back to the cottage after that, poked up the fire and unpacked her few things, then rather resentfully changed into uniform. As she fastened the silver buckle of her petersham belt around her slim waist, she tried to sort out her impressions; so her day had been arranged for her—her free time was presumably to be taken when Professor van Duyl was gracious enough to let her have any. A very arrogant type, she told herself, used to having his own way and bossing everyone around. Well, he had better not try to boss her! She caught up the thick ankle-length cape she had had the foresight to bring with her, huddled into it, and went back to the study. Professor Wyllie was sitting in his chair, his eyes closed, snoring quite loudly. She was debating whether she should go out again and knock really loudly, or sit down and wait for him to wake up, when Professor van Duyl's voice, speaking softly from somewhere close behind her, made her jump. 'He will wake presently, Miss Proudfoot—sit down, won't you?'

But first she turned round to have a look; he was standing quite close with a sheaf of papers in his hand and a pair of spectacles perched on his splendid nose; his dark eyes looked even darker because of them.

She sat, saying nothing, and jumped again when he said: 'You are very small and—er—slight, Sister.' He made it sound as though it were a regrettable error on her part.

She didn't turn round this time. 'Oh, so that's why you don't like me.'

He made an exasperated sound. 'My dear good girl, I have no personal feelings about you; just as long as you do your job properly while you are here.'

Eliza tossed her pretty head. 'You really are…' She spoke in a hissing whisper so that the nice old man behind the desk shouldn't be disturbed, but he chose that moment to open his eyes, and although he smiled at her with evident pleasure, she thought how tired he looked. She was on the point of saying so, with a recommendation to go to bed early that evening, but he spoke first.

'Christian, you have the notes sorted out? Good. We'll deal with those presently.' He got up. 'Now, Eliza, if you will come with us.'

He led the way from the room with Eliza behind him and Professor van Duyl shadowing her from behind. They went first to a small, rather poky room where Mr Peters was busy with his pills and phials.

'Each patient has his own box,' he told Eliza, 'clearly

marked. Syringes and needles here,' he indicated two deep enamel trays, 'injection tray here—for emergency, you understand. Kidney dishes and so on along this shelf. I'll have them all marked by this evening. I'm on the telephone and you can reach me whenever you want. If I'm not here, young Grimshaw will help you.'

He nodded towards a pleasant-faced young man crammed in a corner, checking stock, and he and Eliza exchanged a smile and a 'Hi', before she was led away to what must, at one time, have been the drawing room of the house. It had several tables and desks in it now and a small switchboard. 'Harry,' said Professor Wyllie, waving a friendly hand, 'sees to the telephone—house and outside line. Bert here does the typing and reports and so on and sees to the post.' He crossed the room and opened another door. 'And this is Doctor Berrevoets, our Path Lab man—does the microscopic work, works out trial injections and all that. He's Dutch, of course.'

Unmistakably so, with a face like a Rembrandt painting, all crags and lines, with pale blue eyes and fringe of grey hair encircling a large head. He made some friendly remark to Eliza, and his English, although fluent, was decidedly foreign. She thought him rather nice, but they didn't stay long with him, but went back the way they had come while Professor Wyllie explained that they all slept in the house and that should she ever need help of any kind, any one of them would be only too glad to assist her. He flung open another door as he spoke. 'The kitchen,' he was vague again; obviously it was a department which had no interest for him at all. Hub was there, pressing a pair of trousers on the corner of the kitchen table, and another man with a cheerful face was standing at the sink, peeling potatoes. Eliza smiled at Hub, whom she already regarded as an old friend, and walked over to the sink.

'Did you cook lunch?' she wanted to know.

He had a rich Norfolk accent as well as a cheerful face. 'I did, miss—was it to your liking?'

'Super. Are you a Cordon Bleu or something like that?'

He grinned. 'No such luck, miss, but I'm glad you liked it.'

Outside in the dusty hall again, Professor van Duyl said blandly: 'Well, now that you have the staff eating out of your hand, Sister, we might settle to work.'

She didn't even bother to answer this unkind observation. 'Who does the housework?' she enquired, and was pleased to see the uncertainty on their learned faces. 'Who washes up and makes the beds and dusts and runs the place?'

They looked at each other and Professor van Duyl said seriously: 'You see that size has nothing to do with it, after all. Motherly, we said, did we not?'

His elderly colleague reminded him wickedly, 'No looks, and not young.'

Eliza listened composedly. 'So I'm not what you expected? But excepting for my size, I am, you know.

I can be motherly when necessary and I—I'm not young.' She swallowed bravely. 'You are both quite well aware that I am getting on for twenty-nine.'

Professor Wyllie took her hand and patted it. 'My dear child, we are two rude, middle-aged men who should know better. You will suit us admirably, of that I am quite sure.'

He trotted away down the hall, taking her with him. 'Now, as a concession to you, we will have a cup of tea before visiting the patients.'

Hub must have known about the tea, for he appeared a moment later with a tray of tea things. 'Only biscuits this afternoon,' he apologised in his quaint but fluent English, 'but Fred will make scones for you tomorrow, miss.'

Eliza thanked him and poured the tea, and looking up, caught Professor van Duyl's eyes staring blackly at her; they gleamed with inimical amusement and for some reason she felt a twinge of disappointment that he hadn't added his own apologies to those of his elder colleague.

The Nissen hut was quite close to the house, hidden behind a thick, overgrown hedge of laurel. It looked dreary enough from the outside, but once through its door she saw how mistaken she had been, for it had been divided into ten cubicles, with a common sitting room at the end, and near the door, shower rooms, and opposite those a small office, which it appeared was for her use. She would be there, explained Professor van Duyl, from eight in the morning until one o'clock, take her free time until half past four and then return on duty until eight in the evening.

'The hours will be elastic, of course,' he told her smoothly, 'it may not be necessary for you to remain for such long periods as these and we hope that there will be no need for you to be called at night.'

She looked away from him. What had she taken on, in heaven's name? And not a word about days off—she would want to know about that, but now hardly seemed to be the time to ask.

She met the patients next; they were sitting round in the common room reading and playing cards and talking, and although they all wore the rather anxious expression anyone with asthma develops over the years, they were remarkably cheerful. She was introduced to them one by one, filing their names away in her sharp, well-trained mind while she glanced around her, taking in the undoubted comfort of the room. Warm curtains here, too and a log fire in the hearth, TV in one corner and well stocked bookshelves and comfortable chairs arranged on the wooden floor with its scattering of bright rugs.

'Any improvements you can suggest?' asked Professor Wyllie in a perfunctory tone, obviously not expecting an answer.

'Yes,' she said instantly. 'Someone—there must be a local woman—to come and clean each day. I could write my name in the dust on the stairs,' she added severely. 'The Nissen hut's all right, I suppose the patients do the simple chores so that you can exclude any allergies.'

Both gentlemen were looking at her with attention tinged with respect.

'Quite right,' it was the Dutchman who answered her. 'They aren't to come into the house. For a certain period each day they will take exercise out of doors, under supervision, and naturally they will be subjected to normal house conditions.' He smiled with a charm which made her blink. 'I am afraid that we have been so engrossed in getting our scheme under way for our ten cases that we rather overlooked other things. I'll see if Hub can find someone to come up and clean as you suggest.' He added politely: 'Do you wish for domestic help in the cottage?'

Eliza gave him a scornful look. 'Heavens, no—it won't take me more than half an hour each day.'

As they went back to the study she reflected that it might be rather fun after all, but she was allowed no leisure for her own thoughts, but plunged into the details of the carefully drawn up timetable.

As the time slid by, Eliza saw that she was going to be busier than she had first supposed. Only ten patients, it was true, and those all up and able to look after themselves, but if one or more of them had an attack, he would need nursing; besides that, each one of them had to be checked meticulously, TPR taken twice a day, observed, charted, exercised and fed the correct diet.

There would be exercises too, and a walk each day. She asked intelligent questions of Professor van Duyl and quite forgot that she didn't like him in the deepening interest she felt for the scheme. It was later, when the last case had been assessed, discussed and tidily put away in its folder, that Professor Wyllie said:

'There's me, you know. They did tell you?'

She nodded. 'Yes, sir.'

'Good. I'm not much use if I start an attack, I can tell you—you'll have to act sharpish if it gets too bad. Got a nasty left ventricular failure that doesn't stand up too well...'

She answered him with quiet confidence. 'Don't worry, Professor, I'll keep a sharp eye on you. Do you carry anything around with you or do I have to fetch it from Doctor Peters?'

'Got it with me, Eliza—waistcoat pocket; usually manage to get at it myself before it gets too bad.'

'You're not part of the experiment?' she asked.

'Lord, no. Couldn't be bothered—besides, I'm a bit past such things.' He laughed quite cheerfully although his blue eyes were wistful.

'Come, come,' she said in the half-wheedling, half-bracing tones she might have used towards one of her own patients, quite forgetting that this nice old man was an important and learned member of his profession and not merely someone who needed his morale boosted. 'That's no way to talk, and you a doctor, too.'

'Motherly,' murmured Professor van Duyl, and she detected the faint trace of a sneer in his voice. 'Is there anything else you wish to know, Sister?'

He was dismissing her and she resented it, but she got to her feet.

'Not at present, thanks. I should like to go back to my office—if I may?' She didn't look at him but at Professor Wyllie, who dismissed her with a wave of his hand and 'Dinner at eight o'clock, Eliza.'

The rest of the day she spent with the patients, getting to know them, and when their supper was brought over from the house she served it, just as she would have done if she had been on her own ward at St Anne's. It was almost eight o'clock by the time she got back to the cottage, to find that someone had been in to mend the fire and turn on the table lamp. She tidied herself perfunctorily because she was getting tired, and huddled in her cloak once more, picked up her torch and went up to the house.

The dining room seemed full of men with glasses in their hands. They stopped talking when she went in and stared as Professor van Duyl crossed the room towards her. She eyed him warily, expecting some nasty remark about being late, but she couldn't have been more mistaken; he was the perfect host. She was given a glass of sherry, established beside him, and presently found herself surrounded by most of the men in the room. She had already met them all that afternoon, but there were three missing, someone told her; Harry, the telephonist, who was on duty, Hub and Fred the cook. They would, they assured her, take it in turns to man the switchboard each evening, and what did she think of the local scenery and did she know that there wasn't a shop for miles around, and how long had she been a nurse?

She answered them all readily enough, but presently excused herself and made her way over to the fireplace, where Professor Wyllie was sitting in a large chair, talking to Doctor Peters, who smiled at Eliza nicely as he strolled away. She perched herself on a stool in front of the old man.

'I wanted to tell you that I think I'm going to like this job very much. I spent an hour or so in the hut—what a nice lot of men they are, and so keen to cooperate. It's all rather different from Men's Medical, though. I hope I'll do.' She looked at him a little anxiously.

'Of course you'll do, girl—couldn't have chosen better myself.'

Her lovely eyes widened. 'But I thought it was you…'

He chuckled. 'Let me explain.' And he did. 'So you see, Christian was a little taken aback when you arrived. He was so certain that Eliza Proudfoot would live up to her name—a worthy woman with no looks worth mentioning and—er—mature.'

'Motherly, buxom and tough,' murmured Eliza.

'Exactly. And instead of that he opens the door on to a fairy creature who looks incapable of rolling a bandage.'

'Is that why he doesn't like me?'

The innocent blue eyes became even more so. 'Does he not? He hasn't said so; indeed, he agreed with me that you will suit us admirably—a nice sharp mind and the intelligence to use it, and not afraid to speak out.' He chuckled gently, then went on seriously. 'I must explain that Christian is engaged to be married to a very…' he hesitated, 'high-minded girl—never puts a foot wrong, the perfect wife, I should imagine, and very good-looking if you like her kind of looks.' He glanced at her. 'That's why he chose you, you see. We had a list of names; yours was the only…' he paused again. 'Well, girl, it's a plain sort of name isn't it? but if you will forgive me for saying so, it hardly matches your delightful person. It was a shock to him.'

'Well, that's all right,' Eliza declared in a matter-of-fact voice. 'He was a shock to me and I don't like him either, though of course I'll work for him just as though I did.'

'Honest girl.' He got to his feet. 'Now, let us eat our dinner and you shall tell me all the latest news about St Anne's.'

Dinner was a gay affair because she sat beside Professor Wyllie and Professor van Duyl was at the other end, at the foot of the table. Although she tried not to, every now and then she glanced at him and caught his eyes upon her in an unfriendly stare, his dark face unsmiling. It spurred her on to make special efforts to amuse her companions at table, and by the time they were drinking their coffee, the laughter around her was evident of her success. But she didn't allow this pleasant state of affairs to swamp her common sense; at exactly the right moment she bade everyone a quiet good night and beat an unassuming retreat. But not a solitary one; Professor van Duyl got to the door—despite the fact that he had been at the other end of the room—a fraction of a second ahead of her, and not only opened it but accompanied her through it. She paused just long enough to catch up her cloak and torch from a chair.

'Thank you, sir,' her voice was pleasantly friendly, if cool, 'I have a torch with me. Good night.'

He took it from her, gently, and opened the house door. It was pitch dark outside and cold, and she felt thankful that it wasn't raining, for her cap, a muslin trifle, lavishly frilled, would have been ruined. As they turned the corner of the house she slowed her pace. 'I'm going over to the hut to say good night,' she informed him. 'I said that I would.'

He made no answer, merely changed his direction, and when they reached the hut, opened the door for her and followed her inside.

The men were glad to see her; they were, to her surprise, glad to see her companion too. He seemed a different man all at once—almost, one might say, the life and soul of the party, and his manner towards herself changed too; he was careful to let them all see that she was now a member of the team, to be relied upon, trusted and treated with respect; she was grateful to him for that. It struck her then that whether she liked him or not, she was going to enjoy working for him.

They stayed for half an hour while Eliza made sure that they were all comfortable for the night; that they understood what they were to do if any one of them started to wheeze. 'I'll be over before I go to breakfast in the morning,' she assured them. 'Good night, everyone.'

They left the hut followed by a chorus of good nights and walked in silence to the cottage, and Professor van Duyl unlocked the door for her.

'Someone came in while I was away and made up the fire,' she told him. 'It was kind of them.'

'Hub—I asked him to. I have a key which I keep in my possession, and I hope that you will do the same.'

'Of course. Good night, Professor.' The little lamp on the coffee table cast a rosy glow over her, so that she looked prettier than ever.

He said austerely, 'And you will be good enough to lock your door when you are in the cottage, Miss Proudfoot.'

'Well, of course I shall—at night time, at any rate.'

'During the day also.'

'But that's a bit silly!' She watched his mouth thin with annoyance.

'Miss Proudfoot, I am seldom silly. You will do as you are told.'

'Oh, pooh!' she exclaimed crossly, and without

saying good night, went into the cottage and shut the
door. She had been in the room perhaps fifteen seconds
when she heard the faint tapping on the back window
of the sitting room. A branch, she told herself firmly,
then remembered that when she had looked out of the
window during the afternoon; there had been no tree
within tapping distance. It came again, urgent and persistent. She ran to the door and flung it open, and in a
voice a little shrill with fright, called: 'Oh, please come
back! There's something—someone…'

CHAPTER THREE

EITHER he had not gone away immediately or he had been walking very slowly; he was there, reassuringly large and calm, before Eliza could fetch another breath.

'The back window—someone's tapping. I'm afraid to look.'

He had an irritating way of not answering when she spoke to him, she thought, as she watched him cross the small room in two strides and fling back the curtains. She shut her eyes tightly as he did so; she might be a splendid nurse, a most capable ward Sister and a girl of spirit, but she wasn't as brave as all that. She heard the Professor laugh softly, and opened them again. He had the window open and was lifting a small, bedraggled cat over the sill, a tabby cat, badly in need of a good grooming, with round eyes and an anxious look. She was across the room and had it in her arms before she spoke: 'Oh, what a prize idiot I am! You poor little beast, I never thought...' She looked at the Professor, who was standing, his hands in his pockets, watching her. 'I'm sorry,' she told him, 'calling you back like that—it's a bad start, isn't it, behaving like a coward.'

He didn't laugh, but said quite gently: 'You're not a coward.' He was going to say more than that, she felt sure, but for some reason he didn't; only as his eyes fell on the little cat: 'Shall I take her up to the kitchen with me? Fred and Hub will look after her.'

'Oh, please don't, I'd love to keep her—that's if you don't mind. She'll be someone to talk to.' She had no idea how wistful she sounded. 'She's very thin…' She looked at the small creature for a minute and then back to her companion's impassive face. 'She's going to have kittens,' she stated.

'So I noticed. You will need a box and some old blanket, and she looks in need of a meal. Don't give her too much to begin with—warm milk if you have any.' He put a hand on the door. 'I'll get a box and something to put inside it—I'll be back very shortly.' At the door he turned. 'Lock the door, Miss Proudfoot.'

It was an order, and rather to her surprise Eliza obeyed it without a murmur.

She warmed some milk, the cat tucked under her arm, and gave it to the starving little beast, who lapped it up and mewed for more. Before she could give it there was a knock on the door and when she opened it, the Professor came in, saying as he did so: 'It is foolish of you to open the door without enquiring who is there, Miss Proudfoot. Don't do it again.'

'I shall begin to feel that I'm on Devil's Island if you go on like this,' she told him roundly, but he only smiled slightly.

'I'm responsible for you. Here is a box and the old blanket and Hub sent this—chicken from dinner—I'll cut it very small, for she mustn't eat too much at a time. She drank her milk?'

'Yes.' Eliza was arranging the box near the fire. 'She wanted more.'

He was in the kitchen at the table; she could see him through the open door, bending his great height over the chicken. For no reason at all, she found herself wondering about the girl he was going to marry. High-minded, Professor Wyllie had said. The perfect wife and good-looking to boot; he must have picked her with care—a girl who would never irritate him or forget how important he was, and who wouldn't expect him to run around at night rescuing cats. She set the little beast in the box and called:

'I'll finish that, sir. It was kind of you to fetch it. I'll let her have a little and then she can go to sleep.'

He came back from the kitchen with a saucer of chicken, cut very small, and stood looking down at her. 'By all means give her some, but I should wait until she has had the kittens.' He put the saucer down, threw another log on the fire and pulled up a chair. 'Are you going to stay there on the floor, or would you like a chair?' And when Eliza said she would stay where she was, he sat himself down and stretched his legs out to the blaze. Apparently he intended to remain.

'I'm not frightened of being alone,' she told him.

His dark face was transformed by a charming smile, 'I know you're not,' he assured her, 'but this creature's in a poor state, she might want a little help.'

They sat in silence for a few minutes, and Eliza, peeping at him, saw that he had closed his eyes. They opened immediately at a faint mew from the cat, though, and caught her looking at him, so that she had to look away quickly. There was a black and white kitten in the box. 'Ah, Primus,' declared Eliza, glad of something to talk about. 'Do you suppose she belongs to someone? That village I came through on the way here—she could have come from there.'

'Perhaps, but I doubt if anyone would want her back; she has obviously been on her own for some time. Here's Secundus.' A small tabby had arrived, squeaking loudly. 'I doubt if there will be any more.'

He was right. They sat watching the pathetic little mother, now content and purring, for another ten minutes or so until Eliza asked: 'Should she have something to eat now? The chicken?'

He offered the saucer, and its contents were scoffed with incredible rapidity, as was a second saucer of milk. The cat licked appreciative whiskers and curled herself up tidily, the kittens tucked up against her.

'She's purring again,' said Eliza with satisfaction. 'Isn't that super?' She got to her feet and the Professor got up too, remarking as he went:

'We met only today, and yet it seems as though…' He didn't finish what he had begun to say but bade her a brusque good night, and she was left to puzzle about it, and wonder why he had looked, all of a sudden, so very annoyed. Just as she had decided that he was rather nice after all. As she got ready for bed she found herself envying—in a vague way—the girl he was going to marry.

She got up early the next morning so that she might tidy the cottage and tend to the little cat's needs. The little creature would need a name; Eliza tried out several, but they didn't sound right, but when she gave it a final stroke and called it, for lack of inspiration, Cat, it responded with such pleasure that she gave it that name then and there.

Up at the house as she passed the kitchen, Hub came out to meet her. 'The little cat, miss,' he asked, after a polite good morning, 'shall I feed her for you during the morning?'

She was glad to have that little problem solved for her. 'Oh, Hub, if you would—I left the window open so that she could go in and out, and the kittens are well tucked up. I'll give her a good meal at midday. There are two kittens.'

'So the Professor told me, miss.' He smiled at her in a fatherly fashion and went to open the dining room door for her.

There were several people there at various stages of breakfast, but neither of the professors were at table. Eliza exchanged good mornings, ate a good breakfast with the speed of long custom and went over to the hut. It was only just half past seven and still barely light, but it was her first day; there would be plenty to do and she was bound to be a little slow.

The patients were already up, and mindful of her instructions, she took temperatures, noted what sort of a night they had had and served their breakfast. She had only just finished this when Professor van Duyl came in, wished her an austere good morning and sat down at the breakfast table with his patients, where he stayed for several minutes, talking in Dutch or English as the occasion demanded and drinking the coffee she had thoughtfully poured for him. He went away presently, and when she went to her office she found him there, sitting on a corner of the desk, scrutinising the charts. He didn't look up as she went in, but after a few minutes, asked: 'The cat is well?'

She began to write up the diets, sitting at the desk within inches of him. 'Yes, thank you. I'm going to call her Cat—isn't it fortunate that the men all suffer from extrinsic asthma and not the allergy kind?'

His mouth curved faintly. 'Very, otherwise we would have to have found her a new home.' He looked at his watch and got up go. 'You are confident of the day's routine, Sister?'

She nodded silently, feeling snubbed, and when he had gone, sat down herself, to tidy the desk and read through the notes she had made. The purpose of the whole experiment, Professor Wyllie had told her during the previous afternoon, was to see if something could be done to ease the lot of the asthmatic patient, who, unlike his fellow sufferer, needed no dust or cat fur or pollen to start him off wheezing, only an emotion. One of the men in the group, he had told her, needed only a good laugh to start an attack, and several started to wheeze only when they were confronted with some circumstance which upset them. 'We want to keep them here for a month,' he explained, 'give them a strict, healthy routine to live by with little or no chance of them encountering the causes of their asthma as possible. Build up their mental resistance, as it were. Of course we're bound to have the odd setback—Mijnheer Kok, for example, who starts to wheeze the moment he sets eyes on his mother-in-law, I have known him to go into *status asthmaticus* at the sight of a letter from her. But this research may help a little towards preventing what is a distressing condition.'

And probably he was quite right, she thought, gathering the papers tidily together before going to see if her ten charges were ready for their prescribed walk. At least it wasn't raining; indeed, there had been a touch of frost during the night; a walk would be pleasant. Eliza got her cape and stood looking down at her feet, encased in sensible enough shoes but hardly the thing for a walk in the Scottish Highlands. She was wondering what to do about them when Hub appeared silently at the open door.

'Miss?' He held out a pair of Wellington boots and a pair of knitted gloves. Both were too big but very acceptable. She thanked him nicely, to be told that it had been Professor van Duyl's orders, and would she remember not to go any further than the stream at the end of the rough track behind the house. 'And the post will be here when you get back, miss,' said Hub as he turned to go. 'I have also visited the little cat.'

She enjoyed the walk, going from one group to the next as they went, getting to know them, watching them carefully, taking care to temper the pace so that they wouldn't be overtired. There were pulses to take when they got back, hot mid-morning drinks to give out and the charts to write up carefully; it was surprising how quickly the morning flew by.

And she had a letter too, from her mother. She read it over her coffee, smiling a little because her mother so obviously thought of her job as being rather more orthodox than it was. The men's dinner came over at midday; she served them out, made sure that it was eaten, and afterwards gently chivvied the men to their beds for their rest period. She was free now to go to her own lunch, leaving careful instructions as to where she would be before she did so.

But first she had to go and see Cat. Someone had been there before her; the fire was freshly lighted, a guard set before it, and the little cat with her kittens established in the box within the circle of its warmth. She had been fed too, Eliza noted, that would be Hub again. She stroked her protegée, did her hair and face with speed and went up to the house.

Only Professor Wyllie was there in the dining room. He greeted her cheerfully, explaining that lunch was a moveable feast and that she would have to put up with his company. 'Most of them have eaten,' he told her, 'and Christian has gone down to the village to fetch a woman who might do for the cleaning. Perhaps you would see her presently and tell us what you think— better still, engage her if she suits you.'

Eliza helped herself to an appetizing macaroni cheese. 'Of course. How marvellous to get anyone— however did you manage it?'

'Not me—Christian; went down to make enquiries this morning early—said he'd better get someone before you flew off the handle again.' He chuckled richly and Eliza choked indignantly. 'I never flew…well, perhaps just a bit; the stairs are very dusty,' she pointed out severely.

They didn't talk much, but the long silences were companionable; she liked Professor Wyllie and she suspected that he didn't always feel as fit as he would like people to believe. He was puffing a little and he looked pinched. She said diffidently: 'Professor Wyllie, will you be sure and let me know if there's anything I can do for you at any time?'

The blue eyes were very direct. 'I will, thank you, Eliza. I dare say you will have me on your hands sooner or later. Are you quite comfortable in your cottage? And what's all this about a cat and kittens?'

The rest of the meal passed pleasantly enough; Eliza was on the point of leaving the dining room when the door opened and Professor van Duyl came in. He said without preamble: 'There you are. I have a Mrs MacRae here—I've put her in the sitting room—you had better see if she'll suit you.'

He sounded quite bad-tempered about it and she had half a mind to say so, but there seemed little point; he didn't like her and she would have to accept that fact. A faint flicker of regret about that caused her to shake her head and frown as she went out of the room.

The sitting room was quite nice but hopelessly neglected. No one used it—the two professors and possibly Doctor Peters and Doctor Berrevoets used the study, and there was another smaller room down the hall where the rest of the team went. Mrs MacRae was sitting on the very edge of a chair, registering disapproval, and Eliza could hardly blame her. Someone with a frivolous turn of mind had written: 'Dust me,' on the mirror and there were cobwebs on the walls, and yet it could be a charming room; the furniture was old-fashioned but good and comfortable too. If the carpet were once cleared of dust, and its red serge curtains shaken and brushed and a few flowers here and there... She smiled at Mrs MacRae and said: 'Good afternoon. I'm Eliza Proudfoot, the nurse looking after the patients here. The professor asked me to see you.' She paused hopefully, but all Mrs MacRae said was 'Aye.'

'It's quite a nice house,' said Eliza, trying again, 'but you can see how neglected it is—it was the first thing I noticed, and if I had the time I would give it a good clean, but my days are pretty full. I wondered if you...?'

'Aye,' said Mrs MacRae again, and much emboldened by this monosyllable, Eliza asked: 'When could you come? Just an hour or two each day...'

'The noo. Twa, three hours.'

'Oh, super!' She watched while Mrs MacRae, a small, sandy-haired body with the most beautiful blue eyes in the plainest of faces, opened the large plastic bag on her lap. From it she drew an overall, a cotton head-square and a pair of carpet slippers.

'I say, may I help you?' Eliza felt drawn to the little woman, perhaps because it would be so delightful to have another woman about the place even if only for a few hours a day.

'Aye.' Her companion eyed her uniform. 'Ye'll need a pinny.'

Eliza nodded. There was an apron hanging in the kitchen at the cottage and she could cover her hair with a scarf. 'Where shall we start?' she asked with enthusiasm.

'Upstairs. Is there a broom and such?'

'I'll find everything,' promised Eliza, and flew away.

She was back within minutes, swathed in the apron, her hair tucked away under the scarf, bearing a variety of household appliances. They went upstairs without waste of time and opened the first door they came to—Professor Wyllie's room, the bed neatly made, it was true, but otherwise sorely neglected. Mrs MacRae tut-tutted, gave directions and set to work with Eliza a willing helper. They were bearing the sheepskin rugs downstairs to the garden behind the house when they encountered Professor van Duyl. He flattened himself against the wall to let them pass and when Eliza was level with him remarked nastily: 'You are one of those people who keep a dog and bark yourself, Sister Proudfoot.' He eyed her coldly. 'You are also extremely dirty.'

She paused, and a cloud of dust rose from the rugs she was carrying. 'Pooh,' she declared roundly, 'and you've got the wrong proverb. You mean: "Many hands make light work".'

She gave him a cold look, her lovely face quite undimmed by the layer of dust upon it, and went on down the stairs, out to the rough grass which must, at some time or other, have been a beautiful lawn. They brushed and beat and shook the mats until they reached the perfection both ladies found desirable and bore them back upstairs, and Eliza, who had been uncommonly hard on her rugs, felt much better, although she would have preferred to have banged and thumped Professor van Duyl instead of the sheepskins.

They hung the curtains once more, polished the furniture and stood back to admire their handiwork. The room looked quite different; she doubted if Professor Wyllie would notice anything, but they at least had the satisfaction of knowing that it was shining and spotless.

'Come and have a cup of tea with me,' suggested Eliza. 'You can come as you are and put your things on in the cottage. There's half an hour to spare.' She hardly waited for Mrs MacRae's 'Aye,' but ran downstairs to get back to the cottage and put the kettle on. As she drew level with the kitchen door, however, it opened and Hub stepped out into the hall.

'Fred took the liberty of making some scones,' he said in his fatherly way. 'There's a nice fire burning and the teapot's warming.'

She took the covered plate he was offering her. 'Oh, Hub, you are a dear—and Fred, bless you both, we shall enjoy them. I'll come and thank Fred later.'

The cottage looked homely and welcoming and Cat got out of her box and came to meet her. Eliza gave her a saucer of milk, put the kettle on, took off her apron and scarf, and washed her face and hands; presently she would take a shower before she went on duty, but now there was no time. She was uncovering the plate which Hub had given her, to discover little cakes as well as scones, when Mrs MacRae arrived.

They made an excellent tea, although there wasn't much time. 'How will you get home?' Eliza wanted to know.

'The Professor, in his car. I'll come tomorrow, same time.'

Eliza wondered if he found it annoying to have to drive to and fro each day as she helped her guest tidy herself, and when she was ready, she went with her to the house, to return the plate and thank Fred. Hub was there too and she thanked him for a second time and he accepted her thanks with dignity, thinking privately that it was a pity he couldn't tell her that it was Professor van Duyl who had gone to the kitchen and told him to see that Miss Proudfoot had a good tea provided each day—it would be more than his job was worth to even hint at it, which was a pity, seeing that the pair of them had started off on the wrong foot.

Eliza, who had privately hoped that she might have seen Professor van Duyl when she went up to the house, didn't see him again that day. His elder colleague came down to the hut to talk to his patients during the evening, making copious notes as he did so, and when she went off duty and went up to the house for supper, it was to find no sign of the Dutchman, but Harry was there, sitting opposite her. He called across the table: 'Watcher, sister,' and when she answered him and wanted to know what he was doing, away from his telephone, he told her: "Is Nibs is doing a stint at the switchboard—turns 'is 'and ter anything, 'e does, that man. 'Ow's tricks, Sister?'

She told him readily enough, musing the while over the punctilious way in which everyone addressed her as Sister. It made her feel a little elderly and aloof, and she guessed that it was Professor van Duyl who had instigated it. The conversation became general and lively enough over the excellent supper, only from time to time she found herself glancing down the table to where he should have been sitting, and wasn't, and although she assured herself that it was a great deal nicer without his dark gaze meeting hers each time she raised her head, she was conscious of disappointment.

Sitting by the dying fire in the cottage after her good night round in the hut, she found herself thinking about him again—an ill-tempered, arrogant man, she told Cat, given to wanting his own way. 'I hope,' she observed to the small creature, 'that this paragon of a girl he is going to marry will keep him in his place.'

Cat yawned and took no notice at all, and Eliza said a little crossly:

'Oh, of course you wouldn't agree—he rescued you, didn't he?' She cast the animal a smouldering glance and went to bed.

The ringing of the internal telephone, placed strategically by her bed, wakened her, and when she answered it with a quick 'Yes?' it was one of the Dutchmen, Mijnheer Kok, who wheezed out an agonised 'Sister…'

'I'm coming,' she told him, and hung up. She was in her slacks and an old guernsey, pulled over her nightie, within seconds, with the socks she had charmed out of Hub on her feet and her length of hair tied back with an end of ribbon. The torch and her Wellingtons were by the door; she shoved her feet into their roominess, shone the torch on Cat to make sure that she and the kittens were still safe and sound, and let herself out into the dark. The cold bit her as she turned the key in the lock and slipped it into her pocket; it was almost three o'clock in the morning and freezing.

Mijnheer Kok was sitting up in his bed, gasping in air and then struggling to let it out again, and there was no need, even if he had had the breath, to tell Eliza what was the matter. She nodded at him reassuringly as she switched on the oxygen, took his pulse and then went to the telephone in the office. Professor van Duyl answered her. He listened in silence while she made her brief urgent report, said: 'I'll be with you in a couple of minutes,' and rang off. She was standing by her patient, adjusting the oxygen flow, when she became aware of him, in a tremendously thick sweater and slacks, standing beside her.

'How long?' he asked, and smiled reassuringly at Mijnheer Kok.

'I was called at five minutes to three. I've not asked him any questions.'

He nodded, aware as she was that poor Mijnheer

Kok had no breath for conversation. 'OK,' he handed her an ampoule, 'give him adrenaline 1:1000—0.5 stat.'

Eliza did as she was told, listening to him talking in his own language to Mijnheer Kok. His voice sounded different; there was no coldness in it now; it was unhurried and calm as he took the man's pulse and rolled up his pyjama sleeve, and there was a warmth in it she hadn't heard before. She gave the injection slowly and then picked up the chart to record it while they waited for it to take effect. Only poor Mijnheer Kok showed no signs of improvement; the prescribed half hour dragged by and there was nothing to do but maintain a calm front and see that the oxygen was at its correct volume, but the moment the thirty minutes were up, at a nod from the Professor she drew up another injection and gave that. It was obvious that this wasn't going to help either; another half hour had almost gone when he said: 'I'm going to give amino-phylline—0.25 should do it. A syringe, please, Sister, and ten ml. of sterile water.'

She prepared it and watched while he found a vein and injected it and this time the improvement was dramatic. Mijnheer Kok's labouring chest gradually quieted itself, his breathing became slower and his colour almost normal, and after a little while he smiled at them. Eliza arranged him more comfortably on his pillows and began to tidy up, leaving everything to hand in case it should be needed again. The Professor was talking quietly to his patient, and presently she heard him give a low laugh. 'Kok had a dream about his mother-in-law,' he explained. 'He woke up thinking about her and started wheezing at the very idea. We'll put him on phenobarbitone for a day or two and something last thing to abort any further paroxysm.' He looked intently at his patient. 'He's tired out, he'll sleep now.' He looked at his watch. 'I'll stay the rest of the night in the office.'

Eliza didn't look at him as she straightened the blankets. 'That won't be necessary, thank you, sir. I'll stay, that's what I'm here for.'

'True,' he agreed coolly, 'but if you don't get another hour or two's sleep there will be no one in a fit state to look after the other nine men later.' He gave her a quick detached look and added, 'That's an order, Sister Proudfoot.'

She didn't answer but went obediently to the door, and he added quickly:

'Wait—Kok is asleep and will remain so. I'll walk over to the cottage with you.'

'I'm quite all right, thank you, I'm not nerv…' She could have bitten out her tongue the moment she had said it; only last night she had behaved like a frightened child. But all he said was, in the mildest of voices, 'I know that. All the same, you will allow me to take you back.' He turned back to the sleeping man for a moment, then followed her out of the cubicle.

'I'll just make sure the rest of them are sleeping,' she whispered, and went softly from one man to the other before rejoining him.

It took less than a minute to reach the cottage; he took the key from her and opened the door and switched on the light before standing on one side to allow her to enter. Cat stretched in her box, made a pleasant welcoming sound and walked to meet them, leaving the kittens in a sleeping heap. She passed Eliza with a mere flick of her tail and went to wreathe her small body round the Professor's long legs.

'Ungrateful wretch!' exclaimed Eliza. 'I'm the one who feeds you and gives you a home.' She yawned unaffectedly like a small girl and turned to wish her companion a good night—not that there was much night left by now. Bed, with a hot water bottle and possibly a hot drink. The idea of the Professor sitting over in the hut pricked her conscience. 'Look,' she said quickly, 'let me go back—you'll be so tired.'

A strange look came over his face. He said slowly: 'That is kind of you, but I shall be quite all right. It will be better if you do your full duty tomorrow, you are more necessary than I.'

Bed making, she thought, and seeing that the men were warmly clad and weren't too hot and did their breathing exercises, and all the other small, necessary chores. He was right, of course. 'Well, would you like a hot drink? Have you time?'

He had picked up Cat and was stroking her small, large-eared head.

'That would be nice, thank you.'

'Well, sit down. There's still a little warmth in the ashes—the kettle won't take long.'

She left him to go into the kitchen and make tea, and presently came back with a tray and a tin of biscuits beside. When she had poured him a cup and given Cat a saucer of milk she took a sip from her own cup and asked: 'Hell be all right now?'

'Kok? I think it unlikely that he will have another attack in the immediate future, if he does we must try him with Prednisolone—we don't want *status asthmaticus*, do we? Tranquillisers may help. We'll try for a day or so and I'll talk to him—if I can convince him that his stay here, away from everyone, will contribute to the lessening of his attacks, we might manage to control them to a certain extent.'

'Inject him, as it were, with an anti-emotion.'

His dark eyes snapped. 'You understand. I have tried it once or twice in Holland with success and Professor Wyllie has done the same thing over here. This is the field of psychology, of course, but we both feel strongly that the family doctor or a specialist with whom the patient is familiar is more suited to such work.'

'Have you a practice?'

He hesitated slightly. 'Yes—in Nijmegen.' He got up, towering over her in the small room. 'I must go back to Kok.' His voice, which had been warmly friendly, had become indifferent again; he was all of a sudden anxious to be gone. 'Thank you, Sister.'

His glance raked her and a smile tugged at the corner of his mouth and she knew why. Anyone looking less like a hospital Sister would be hard to find. The guernsey was on its last legs, her slacks were stuffed into the Wellingtons and her hair, escaped from its hastily tied ribbon, hung curly and untidy, around her face. She said with tremendous dignity:

'Don't mention it, sir. Thank you for coming over.' She ushered him to the door, wished him a brisk good night and shut the door smartly behind him. As she cleared away the tea tray and filled her hot water bottle, she told Cat exactly what she thought of him. 'And if he wants to snub me whenever I open my mouth,' she explained to the listening animal, 'then he shan't have the chance!'

As from that very day, she decided, huddling into bed and shivering a little, she would give him no opportunity to talk. No more cups of tea and certainly no more light chat about his work in Holland. She would say 'Yes, sir,' and 'No, sir,' and keep out of his way. As she drifted off into sleep she realized that she was sorry about this, but she was far too tired to go into her feelings more deeply.

CHAPTER FOUR

SHE was up at her usual time in the morning, and after attending to Cat's small wants, went over to the hut. It was early still, and she had quite forgotten her resolution to keep out of Professor van Duyl's way; it was something of a shock to find him still there, sitting by Kok's bed. He had been writing, for there were a number of closely written sheets scattered round his chair, but now he was sitting doing nothing, his dark features rendered darker still by reason of the stubble on his chin and the deep lines of tiredness running between his handsome nose and mouth. That his thoughts were far away was evident; perhaps with the girl he was going to marry. Eliza frowned as she thought it—she was allowing her mind to dwell too much on him and his affairs. She wished him a good morning in a cool voice and offered to make him a cup of tea, which he refused with a curtness which verged upon rudeness.

'Let him sleep,' he told her, nodding towards Kok. 'If

he wakes before I get back, give him a light breakfast.
I shall return before you go with the men for the
morning exercise.'

And he did, freshly shaved, the tired lines miracu-
lously gone, and as immaculate as though he had
enjoyed a good night's sleep and all the time in the
world in which to dress. She wondered how he did it—
and presumably he had had his breakfast too.

Beyond telling him that she had left coffee warming
on the hot plate in the day room, she said nothing. Mr
Kok was still sleeping quietly, the men were ready to go
out; Eliza put on her cape and boots and went with them.

She helped Mrs MacRae again that afternoon; after
all, there was a great deal to do, more than one person
could manage, though once they had turned the house
out thoroughly, a daily clean through, which Mrs
MacRae would be able to manage on her own, would
suffice. She followed the stalwart little woman upstairs
once more and into a bedroom, as dusty as the first one
had been but considerably tidier, only on a small table
drawn up under a window there was a hotchpotch of
papers, closely written notes, and open books. Professor
van Duyl's room, Eliza guessed, and had the guess confirmed by the sight of a framed photograph of a young
woman, placed, she couldn't help but notice, where it
could be seen from every corner of the room. She had
no chance to look at it immediately, but later, when Mrs
MacRae had gone downstairs with the rugs, leaving her

to get on with the polishing, she took the photograph to the window so that she might study it. Professor Wyllie had been right; here was a very handsome young woman, with classical features and wearing the air of one who would never allow anyone or anything to upset her calm. Insipid, nonetheless decided Eliza, despite the fact that she had the appearance of a person who was always right and took care to tell you so.

She didn't know what made her look over her shoulder. The Professor was standing in the doorway watching her, his face sombre with some emotion she had no time to guess at. She turned round to face him, still clutching the photograph, her face pink, and she found that when she came to speak that she had lost most of her breath.

'You don't mind?… You must think me very inquisitive… She's so very good-looking.'

He glared down his splendid nose. 'Since you have taken upon yourself the work of a housemaid as well as that of nurse, and have access to my room, it would appear useless for me to mind.'

She fidgeted under the chilly voice and the even chillier look; surely there was no need to be so scathing? She decided to ignore it. 'But she is very good-looking,' she persisted. 'Is she your fiancée?'

She thought he wasn't going to answer. 'Yes. Tell me, Sister Proudfoot, have you no prospects of marriage?'

It seemed a funny way of putting it, and the tone of

his voice suggested that she must be lacking in something or other. She said quite sharply: 'Of course I have—but I've never met a man I wanted to marry.'

A lie, she realized that even as she uttered it. Of course she had met him; he was here, staring down at her through the glasses he had seen fit to put on, fiercely frowning at her through them and behaving as though he couldn't stand the sight of her. She felt bewildered at the suddenness of her discovery and looked back at him, her pretty mouth a little open.

'You stare, Sister.' His voice had an edge to it; it caused her to close it with a snap and pulled her tumbling wits together. It seemed to her extraordinary that he hadn't seen…that he could be unaware of the strength of the feelings bottled up inside her and screaming to give utterance… She must look the same as usual; the thought was capped by his: 'You are as dirty and untidy as you were yesterday. Must you really do this work? You ask for someone to clean the house and then you do most of it yourself?'

At least her thoughts were diverted. She explained carefully about there being too much work for Mrs MacRae, and added: 'Once we've done it all thoroughly, she'll be able to manage nicely on her own. And I don't mind.'

He smiled, a thin, half-sneering smile which made her wince. 'That is beside the point. You were not asked to do housework; if you choose to do it, that is entirely your own affair and certainly not my business.'

He turned on his heel and walked away, and although she saw him later at supper, he had nothing to say to her.

The days slid past until they made a week. Eliza had the routine nicely organised now; she knew the men and their small fads and fancies, she knew, instinctively, when any one of them was verging on an attack. With the first look of apprehension and the first wheeze, she pounced with the ephedrine or the isoprenaline, summoned one of the professors, and had the sufferer nicely propped up in a chair by the time someone arrived, ready to be talked out of further wheezes, and if that were not possible, ready for whatever treatment was ordered. The men had come to trust her as well as like her, and seeing how they had improved and become relaxed under the strict régime in which they lived, she spent more time with them than was strictly required of her.

By the end of the week, too, the house cleaning had been finished; she was no longer needed, Mrs MacRae told her, adding thanks for the help she had received, but she still came each day and had a cup of tea with Eliza in the cottage, not talking much, but pleased to be there. And Cat had fattened up nicely, fed by the entire community; she found that she had time to herself now— an hour or two each afternoon, and once or twice Professor Wyllie had come down to the hut after tea and sent her off duty, declaring that if he needed her he could get her quickly enough. She spent pleasant hours by the fire, with Cat and her kittens at her feet, writing

letters and reading, and one evening, because she had
felt like it, she had changed into a high-necked jersey
dress in a pleasing shade of brown, and taken pains
with her hair and face; it had been gratifying to feel the
little stir it had created amongst the rest of the staff, only
Professor van Duyl had looked at her as though she had
no right to be there. And about him, she had come to
terms with herself; he didn't like her and he was going
to marry another girl; these two facts alone made it
amply clear that even if she had set out to engage his
interest, she would have had no chance, and the alternative was clear; to go on as she was going now for
another three weeks or so, and then, after that, to forget
him. It was a little difficult to keep to this resolve, but
she felt that she was doing rather well; she was certainly
learning to keep out of his way, and unless he was in the
hut, that wasn't too difficult, and in the hut they were
both on the job and things were different.

The weather was beginning to change; the rain had
given way to light frost and occasional clear skies, but
the wind seemed to increase each day. Eliza sat in her
cottage, listening to it whistling and sighing, and
wondered what it would be like if it should blow a gale,
and well into the second week the rain returned and
combining with the wind, made it impossible for the
men to go out, so that other forms of exercise had to be
devised—mild drill, deep breathing and steady
marching round the cleared day room took up an hour

or more of each morning, with Mr Grimshaw acting as instructor and Eliza keeping a close eye on pulses and respirations. It made a nice change.

It was after two days of this weather that she wakened in the night to hear the rain pelting down, and when she went outside in the morning, it was to find a water-logged path and pools of water in all the hollows. It rained again during the morning, a steady downpour from a black sky which turned with frightening sudden-ness to a torrential downpour. Eliza, mindful of her patients' aptitude to wheeze if they became worried or anxious, settled them round the table with a Monopoly board, pulled the curtains against the disturbing world outside, and went to join them. It was almost dinner time for the men; presumably someone would telephone from the house and tell her what to do about it, for it was certainly no weather in which to go out.

Professor van Duyl didn't share her views, however. He appeared not five minutes later, in oilskins and a sou'wester, his feet in Wellingtons, all of which he dis-carded, together with a couple of large cans.

'Stew,' he explained laconically, 'potatoes in the other one.' He went back to the oilskins and fished around in one of its pockets, to produce two cardboard cartons. 'Eggs—Fred is sure you can make omelettes.'

He carried the whole lot to the other end of the room where the hot plate was and without another word went to take her place at the table while Eliza put the cans to

heat and went in search of a bowl and a frying pan,
thanking heaven silently that omelettes were something
she was rather good at.

They laid the table between them presently, and when
the Professor gave himself a plate, she filled it with
stew before taking some for herself and sitting down to
eat it quickly so that she might get started on the omelettes. It was a laborious business, what with only having
a small bowl and a fork to do the beating, but she
managed well enough, with the men laughing and
joking and assuring her that she was a marvellous cook,
and when they had all finished, she carried everything
out to the sink beside the office and did the washing up
with more helpers than she really needed. Only the
Professor didn't come near her; he went into the office,
and she could hear him talking on the telephone in his
own language and longed to know who it was.

The rain ceased abruptly and he went away to fetch
Mrs MacRae, warning her to walk carefully when she
went over to the cottage, a walk she hardly relished, but
the men were comfortably tucked up for the afternoon
and there was nothing for her to do; she put on her cape
and boots and went outside, where she found it still
raining although the sky had become lighter and it
seemed to her that the wind had gathered strength. The
path to the cottage was water-logged and outside the
front door it was trickling slowly down the hill, but
inside it was warm and dry. It was nice to find the fire

alight and Cat's dinner—the tastiest bits from the kitchen—left on the table. She fed her, changed into slacks and a sweater and turned on her small radio. Gales, said a voice, and heavy rain and more gales; those living in certain areas should beware of flooding. She poked the fire to a greater warmth, kicked off her shoes and toasted her feet as she started on a letter home. She had written half of it when she became aware of Cat's strange behaviour; she had got out of her box and was carrying a kitten off to the bedroom. Presently she came back and took the second one too, and Eliza, intrigued, got up quietly and followed her. All three of them were in the centre of the bed and Cat was making anxious noises.

'Well, whatever's the matter with you?' enquired Eliza. 'Surely it's warm enough by the fire? And you can't be hungry; you've only just had your dinner.'

But Cat was looking anxious, so Eliza went back to her chair—but on the way something stopped her. There was water seeping in under the door—just a gentle ooze, spreading lazily, so that it lapped first the door mat and then crept round its edges to inch its way over the brick floor towards the rush matting which covered the greater part of it. Eliza went to the door and had a look, taking the precaution of putting on her boots first, which was a good thing; the path outside was no longer a path but a small, swift-running river, channelling its way through the rough ground on its way downhill. As she stared, another surge of water washed under the door; no wonder Cat had removed herself and her kittens so prudently.

'You might have told me!' cried Eliza, whipping the doormat out of the way, rolling back the matting and starting to move the furniture away from that end of the room. The water was coming in steadily now and she stood uncertainly for a few moments, watching it. But standing and looking at it wouldn't help and it might not get any worse; she could at least get rid of what she'd got. She fetched the large old-fashioned broom from the kitchen and opened the door again, defiantly sweeping the water out as fast as it came in. She was still engaged in this unrewarding task when Professor van Duyl arrived, wading down the path, a broad plank of wood over one shoulder. He brushed past her, put the plank down and started to take off his oilskins.

'Beastly weather,' he observed mildly, a remark which set her off laughing, so that she stopped work with the broom and the water she had swept out came creeping in again.

'What's that for?' she asked, nodding at the board.

'To stop the water coming in, of course. But you'll need to get all this out of the place first.'

She handed him the broom. 'You're bigger than I am—you sweep, I'll start mopping up.'

A look of surprise swept over his face, followed by amusement.

'You can use a broom, I suppose?' she wanted to

know. She put it into his hand, and not stopping to see
whether he could or not, went back into the kitchen to
find a bucket and floor-cloth.

The little room looked a mess and it was hard to
know where to begin, but at least her companion was
making headway against the flood. He shot the worst
of it through the door, flung down the broom and
rammed the plank across the door, put on his gear once
more and went outside to stand in the water, patiently
wedging stones against it to hold it firm.

Eliza picked up the broom and put it tidily away, then
got down on her knees. The bricks were covered in a
thin film of mud with puddles in the crevices, and it was
a dirty job; she mopped and squeezed and changed the
filthy water, and presently, his job done outside, the
Professor joined her. He was a little awkward at it to
begin with, but before long he was going as fast as she
was. They wrung the last muddy drops from their cloths
and she said kindly: 'You're quite good at it—you must
have had a very sensible mother.'

He blinked rapidly. 'Er—yes, though I can't
remember…'

'Well, I don't suppose you can,' she interrupted impatiently. 'What I mean is, she brought you up to be
handy about the house—boys should be able to make
themselves useful.'

He said yes meekly and offered to empty the bucket
while she boiled the kettle. 'For the floor will have to

be scrubbed before the mat goes back,' she explained, 'but you can have some hot water first and wash. There's hot water in the shower, but it's difficult to get at unless you don't mind getting wet all over.'

He said nothing to this, only waited until she had filled her bucket with hot soapy water, then took it from her and went back into the sitting room, where he patiently mopped the floor dry as she scrubbed it. With two of them it didn't take long. They left it to dry out and went back to the kitchen, where they cleared away the mess and washed at the kitchen sink. 'Where's Cat?' asked the Professor suddenly.

'On my bed—with the kittens, of course. She took them there just before I saw the water coming in— wasn't she clever? Is the house flooded too?'

'No. It stands on a rise, you know, and so does the hut, you're the only one—the entire manpower in the place was poised to come and rescue you. I said I'd take a look and let them know if I needed more help.'

She was drying her hands on a muddy towel, her face rosy with her efforts, her hair slipping from its pins. 'How kind of them all, and thank you for coming. I should have been all right, but it's so much quicker with two. Would you like a cup of tea?'

She ushered him back into the sitting room and told him to make himself comfortable. 'Though you might put a log or two on the fire first,' she suggested. 'It's only biscuits, I'm afraid. Hub always has a plate of cakes or scones ready for me in the afternoons—he's really very kind. Did you know him before you came here?'

A peculiar expression crossed the Professor's fine features. He stooped to poke the fire and throw on another log. 'Yes—he's a very good chap.' He strolled back to the kitchen. 'Do you want Cat brought back?'

She spooned the tea into a well warmed pot and added the boiling water.

'Well, what do you think? Will she feel safe, do you suppose?' She turned to look at him enquiringly. 'It won't do it again, will it?'

'I doubt it. It was the burn at the top of the ridge which overflowed, I imagine, and most of it will have gone down the other side of the hill—this was only an outlet for the surplus.'

He carried the tray to the fire and put it on the table by one of the chairs. 'This is very pleasant,' he observed, and sounded faintly surprised as he said it. Not quite his way of life, thought Eliza shrewdly, she doubted if he had ever in his life before taken tea in his socks and muddy slacks and sweater, with an equally grubby hostess to pour out for him. She tucked her stockinged feet out of sight and lifted the teapot.

It seemed strange that they should be sitting together, talking amicably about this and that, just as though they were old friends, when probably the next time they met he would flatten her with some nasty chilling remark. It would have been fun to have asked him about his life in Holland and especially about the girl he was going to marry, even if it would be turning the knife in the wound, but at least she would know something about him, something to remember…now she could only guess. She ventured: 'Is Nijmegen a big city?'

His dark eyes flickered over her face and then looked away. 'Not very. Two hundred thousand people, perhaps. Charlemagne lived there. Once upon a time it was an imperial city of the Hanseatic Empire. The country around is charming and we have a splendid park and an open-air theatre.' He fell silent; apparently these few sparse facts were deemed sufficient to stay her curiosity. She had her mouth open to ask more questions when he asked abruptly: 'And you, Eliza, where do you live?'

He had never called her by name before. She had always disliked it very much, but he had made it sound pretty. She sighed, not knowing it, and said: 'In a small town called Charnmouth, in Dorset. It's really only one main street with a handful of turnings off it. It's close to the sea though, and the coast is very grand, you know, cliffs and a pebbly shore, though there's some sand too. People come in the summer, but not very many, and in the winter it's quiet and very peaceful.' She sighed again, this time with a tinge of homesickness.

'Your parents?' he prompted.

'The house is in the main street at the top of the town, where the road turns round to go to Lyme Regis. My father's retired now—he was in the Civil Service—

he collects fossils; there are heaps on the beach, but I never know them from stones. My mother's just as useless at it.'

He smiled. 'You go home often? In your little car, perhaps?'

'Yes—once a month for a long weekend and for almost all of my holidays.' She paused, seeing her home in her mind's eye. 'It's quite different from the country round here.'

'You like it here?'

'Very much, now that the house is cleaned, and once the weather clears a little, I intend to go walking.'

He put down his cup. 'If you do, I suggest that you take a companion, at least for the first time. It is easy enough to get lost around here; there are no roads to speak of, and very few lodges like this one—Glencanisp Forest stretches for several miles, and although Canisp and Suilven are several miles away, there is plenty of rough hilly country in which to go astray.'

'You know this part of the Highlands?'

He stood up. 'I've been here before.'

Their pleasant little truce was over. He had become all at once distant, even impatient to be gone. She got up too, looking absurdly small without her shoes, and accompanied him to the door. The floor was quite dry again, and a still fast-moving riverlet outside rushed past the board, leaving the cottage dry. He stepped over it and turned to look down on her. 'Thanks for the tea.'

Eliza stared back at him, craning her neck. 'I enjoyed it,' she told him, and smiled delightfully. She was quite unprepared for his sudden swoop. 'My God, so did I,' he said, so softly that she barely heard him, and kissed her hard.

He strode off without another word, leaving her to shut the door and wash the tea things. 'Well, he may be a learned professor,' she told Cat, 'but he certainly knows how to kiss!' She stacked the cups and saucers dreamily, trying to reconcile that kiss with the austere calm of the girl in the photograph. Did she come alive under it, Eliza wondered, as she herself had done, or did that chilly calm remain unmoved? She hoped not, for the Professor's sake. And could that be the reason for his cold ill-humour? she wondered.

She went back on duty presently, to find that the rain had ceased at last, and although the paths were still awash, the worst of the flooding was over. Doctor Berrevoets came over that evening to take blood samples, so that she was kept moderately busy until supper time, and once in the dining room she was bombarded with enquiries as to how she had fared that afternoon. She gave a lighthearted account of it all, saying almost nothing about Professor van Duyl, who wasn't there anyway. He came in late, greeted everyone quietly, wished her a pleasant good evening, just as though he hadn't seen her for a long time and didn't much mind if he didn't see her again, and sat down to eat his supper. It was young Grimshaw who walked over to the hut with her after the meal and stayed while she saw to the men for the night. She wished him a friendly goodnight at the cottage door and locked herself in as he squelched away up the path to the house. Even with Cat and the kittens, it seemed lonely in the room. Eliza sat in her chair and closed her eyes and tried to imagine that the Professor was sitting opposite her, but it was of no use. She got up and started to undress, telling herself impatiently that she was being a fool; a bracing opinion which did nothing to prevent her from bursting into tears.

CHAPTER FIVE

PERHAPS it was because Professor van Duyl persisted in treating her, during the next few days, with a chilling politeness which forbade any but the most necessary conversation being held between them, that she decided to spend her next free afternoon exploring. It was a pity that the very day she had had this idea, she had already committed herself to an afternoon of table tennis with young Grimshaw; a pleasant enough way in which to spend an hour or two, but William seemed very young; she found herself comparing him with Christian van Duyl, an exercise which did nothing to improve her mood. She let William win and went back to a solitary tea with no one for company but Cat and the kittens, for Mrs MacRae had gone home early.

By the following afternoon, after a morning of snubs from the Professor, she was ripe for rebellion. It was a cold day, the sky grey and strangely quiet—a little frightening, she had to admit to herself as she changed into slacks and a thick sweater and crammed her anorak on top. If it hadn't been for the wretched man vexing her so much, she would never have dreamed of going. She fed Cat, tied a scarf over her hair, and set off, waving to Mijnheer Kok, who was looking out of his window as she went past the hut. It was colder than she had thought, and the sky, now that she was in the open and could see it properly, was full of wind clouds and getting darker by the minute. Common sense told her to turn round and go straight back to the warmth of the cottage, but the memory of Christian van Duyl's face, darkly disapproving, acted as a spur to her ill-judged plan. She reached the stream, still swollen from the rain, crossed it safely and began to climb steadily, up the narrow, ill-marked path which would lead her to the edge of the forest. Looking back, she could still see the Lodge; there were one or two lights burning already and they gave her some degree of comfort as she looked at them before continuing her climb. It really was extraordinarily quiet; the sort of quiet before a storm, she thought uneasily, and once again the Professor's dark face, imprinted indelibly beneath her eyelids, prevented her from turning back.

She went on steadily, stopping to look around her from time to time, secretly glad to see that the Lodge was still in sight, but it wouldn't be for much longer; the pewter-coloured sky was covering itself with racing clouds, so low that already some of the higher ground was out of sight, and there was a sudden roaring in the air which made her stop and look about her once more in bewilderment. Wind—a great gale of it—sprang up at the wink of an eye and filling the world with noise, tearing at the shrubs and trees, whistling in and out of the nooks and crannies.

Eliza took shelter under an overhanging ledge of rock, waiting for it to pass, only it didn't—it gathered strength, and the low clouds came even lower so that she was almost immediately enveloped in them. It was like being in a thick fog; she stayed where she was, fighting panic, for suddenly the world was blotted out and she didn't dare to move. The path she had been climbing had been safe enough if one could see where one was going, but now she could slip so easily, or step over the edge and fall down the rock-strewn slopes; besides, now that she could see nothing at all, she hadn't the faintest idea where the Lodge lay; downhill, that she knew, but it would be an easy thing to walk past it in this strange blank world and as far as she remembered from the map, there were no villages in that direction, only Inverkirkaig, and that was on the coast, on the road which ran through the valley. She would have to stay where she was and hope for the weather to improve.

But it didn't, it became a good deal worse; the wind, which had been bad enough, became a demoniacal monster screaming and wailing round her, so that there was no other sound, and now it brought with it short

flurries of soft snow. It settled remorselessly on her so
that the faster she brushed it away, the faster it blanketed
her. She pressed her small person closer to the rock, for
at least the overhanging ledge gave her some protection,
telling herself that she was in no danger, just wet and
cold and longing for a cup of tea. She was frightened
too, although she didn't choose to admit that even to
herself, but half-remembered tales of people getting lost
in blizzards kept crowding into her head and it was difficult not to dwell on the vast area of rough, unlived-in
country around her. She was, she reminded herself brac-
ingly, only a short distance from the Lodge. The
moment the snow stopped she would be able to see its
lights. She gave a small scream as a tearing, rending
sound close by, louder even than the wind, warned her
that a tree had been blown down, but not, thank heaven,
below her—the idea of negotiating a fallen tree on the
way back held no appeal.

She had lost all count of time by now; she could
think only of the warm little cottage with Cat purring
contentedly as they shared their tea. Rather belatedly
she wished that she had told someone where she was
going. True, Mijnheer Kok had seen her, but he was
hardly likely to say anything, and unless someone
visited the hut that evening she might quite well not be
missed until supper time, for the patients might suppose
her to have the rest of the day free. She frowned;
probably by now it was long past her usual time to

return to duty. There would be no one to check the men's pulses or take their temperatures—and supposing one of them started to wheeze? The thought was so disquieting that she left the rock face and took a step or two on to the path, only to discover that it would be impossible for her to go anywhere or do anything; the wind would bowl her over for a start. She retreated, pressing herself against the rock once more, stamping her feet to keep the circulation going and almost jumping out of her skin when another tree came crashing down, bringing with it a shower of earth and stones and grass flying through the dark. There was no point in pretending that she wasn't frightened any more; she was scared stiff, and if she stayed where she was she would be frozen solid, and no one would ever find her.

She was wrong. 'Little fool!' shouted the Professor in such a tremendous voice that he outmatched the wind. He had come upon her with a suddenness to take her breath, which was a good thing, for she had none left to scream with and she would undoubtedly have screamed. All she managed was a thread of a voice: 'Oh, Christian—I've been so frightened!' Even as she said it she thought what a splendid opportunity it was for him to deliver her a lecture, only he didn't; he took her in his arms and held her close, huge and warm and safe in his sheepskin jacket. She had never felt so secure. Nor so happy. She shouted into his shoulder: 'How did you know I was here?'

'I watched you from my window. As soon as you are a little warmer, we will go back.'

She shivered violently. 'I can't…there's a thick mist…you can't see.'

'I know the way, it's perfectly safe.' His voice, though raised against the wind, sounded completely matter-of-fact, and because of that she made a great effort to pull herself together. 'I'm quite warm,' she told him, 'and I'm ready when you are.'

He grunted, took her hand in his and started down the path with Eliza a little behind him. It wasn't quite dark now that they were out from under the ledge, but the mist was just as thick, eddying violently to and fro at the mercy of the wind, but she kept her eyes on his vague dark shape inches away from her nose and stumbled along, slipping and sliding on the loose stones, expecting every moment that she would step into nothingness but knowing in her heart that Christian would never let that happen.

It was like walking through eternity; she was on the point of screaming to him that she couldn't bear another moment of it when she felt round smooth stones under her boots and realized that they were crossing the stream. The stepping stones, although large and flat, were awash with water; she could feel its iciness through her thick boots—it would be very cold if she were to slip. She shuddered strongly and felt his hand tighten reassuringly on hers.

The rough track back to the lodge was gloriously familiar under her feet and Christian had his torch out now, lighting their way, for here, lower down, the mist wasn't quite so thick. He pulled her close beside him as he stopped outside the cottage and held out his hand for the key. Eliza gave it to him silently and he opened the door, pushed her gently inside and closed it again, leaving her standing there in the cosy little room, wet and shivering and quite bewildered. She shed her clothes, had a hot shower and dressed quickly. She was due, she saw to her amazement, on duty in ten minutes—what had seemed like forever up there on the side of the hills had been only the matter of an hour.

She fed Cat, made herself some tea and sat down to drink it before the fire. The Professor had been angry, of course, that was why he hadn't spoken or given her a chance to thank him. It was just as well that she hadn't been able to see his face—had he not called her a little fool?—and yet he had held her so gently. She would have to find him at supper time and thank him, even if it meant a telling off from him, and it would, and what was more, she was honest enough to admit that she would deserve every word of it. She poured more tea, thinking dolefully that if she had wanted to annoy him deliberately she had certainly succeeded.

None of the patients knew of her afternoon's adventure, only Mijnheer Kok remarked that she couldn't have got very far in such a violent storm. She went about her evening duties outwardly as composed as usual, but inside she was in a tumult; for one thing, she hadn't quite recovered from her fright, and for another she was trying to compose a suitable speech of thanks to offer Professor van Duyl when she next saw him.

But there was little opportunity; supper was a haphazard affair, for the gale had blown down the telephone wires connecting the hut to the house, and there was a good deal of coming and going and shouting for tools and torches. Only the two professors and Doctor Berrevoets and Doctor Peters were at the table, and Doctor Peters, who never had much to say for himself anyway, did no more than smile at Eliza and murmur something she didn't catch, leaving the learned gentlemen at either end of the table to carry on any conversation, and that constantly interrupted. It was Professor Wyllie who did most of the talking, making mild little quips about her disastrous walk, pithy remarks about the abominable weather, and a rather rambling discourse about electronics, which as far as she could make out had nothing to do with anyone present. Professor van Duyl, beyond the briefest of comments when his colleague paused for breath, remained silent, although he paid meticulous attention to her wants. They were having coffee when she plucked up sufficient courage to ask him if he would spare her five minutes of his time.

His glance was brief and wholly impersonal. 'Certainly, Sister. In the study, perhaps?'

But Professor Wyllie had a better idea. 'No, you two stay here, we have a small problem to solve and we shall need the desk.'

So they were left to themselves and Eliza, glancing nervously at her companion, thought that he looked bored as well as impatient, a view confirmed the moment the door had been shut.

'And what can I do for you, Sister Proudfoot? I also have several matters to attend to...'

She said quite crossly: 'No doubt. I shan't keep you a moment longer than I need to, but I must thank you for saving me this afternoon; I think that I should have died out there if you hadn't come. I—I would have thanked you sooner, but you didn't give me the chance.'

'I wonder why you went in the first place?' he enquired in a surprisingly mild voice. 'I remember telling you most distinctly not to go too far away on your own—or are you so pig-headed a young woman that you decided that you knew best? Not so young either,' he added suavely.

Eliza had braced herself to take his reprimand with suitable meekness, but now she forgot all about that. 'Don't you know that it's rude to say things like that?' she demanded in a strong voice. 'How dare you remind me that I'm—I'm...'

'Past your first youth?' He was laughing at her. 'My

dear good girl, much you would care what opinion I have of you, you must be well aware that you could pass for an eighteen-year-old girl.'

She forgot for the moment that they were quarrelling. 'Oh, do you really think so?' she asked him. 'Other people have said that to me sometimes, but I've never really believed them.'

'By other people I presume you mean other men, and should I be flattered that you believe me?'

'Oh, yes,' she answered him seriously. 'You see, you don't like me, so it's not flattery.'

He stared at her, his eyes very black. 'What a child you are!'

She frowned. 'Don't be silly, you've just been reminding me that I'm getting on a bit.'

'Age has nothing to do with it,' he told her, and his voice had become austere, 'but you will oblige me, Eliza, by not trailing off on your own in that irresponsible fashion. Supposing no one had seen you?'

'Why were you watching me?'

She thought he was never going to answer. 'I was standing by my window,' he said at length. His voice became quite level and brisk. 'And now if you have nothing more to say, I will see you back to the cottage.'

She was on her feet and making for the door, where she paused long enough to exclaim: 'Anyone would think that you were trying to make me dislike you even more than I do already—and I don't want your

company.' Two palpable lies uttered with such fierceness that they sounded true.

He took no notice of her at all; by the time Eliza
had caught up her cloak from the chair in the hall, he
was beside her, opening the door and ushering her out
into the cold dark, his torch casting a cheerful beam
on the sodden path beneath their feet. And at the
cottage door, when he had unlocked it and given the
key back into her hand, he stood aside to let her go in
and went on standing there, letting in large quantities
of icy wind and swirling mist. Despite his size and
self-assurance, he looked lonely. Risking a snub, she
asked: 'Shall we bury the hatchet long enough for me
to make us some tea?'

His sombre face broke into a smile whose charm
sent her heart thudding. 'I do like a sporting enemy,' he
told her, then came in and shut the door. She left him to
mend the fire while she went to put the kettle on,
thinking as she did so that she would give anything in
the world for him not to think of her as his enemy. She
carried the tray back to the sitting room and found him
by the fire, with Cat and the kittens, wrapped in their
blanket, in a somnolent heap on his knee. Eliza filled a
mug and put it handy for him. 'Do you have cats of your
own?' she asked.

'Two, and Magda, my housekeeper, has one of her
own. I have a dog too, an Alsatian.'

Eliza sipped her tea. 'We had a black retriever, but

he died last year—of old age. Father would like another dog, but he and Mother can't bear the thought of it just yet. I like animals round the house, don't you?'

'Indeed yes, I intended to have a second dog, but Estelle, my fiancée, doesn't care for animals, so it hardly seems fair to add to those I already have.'

She remembered Estelle's calm photographed face; no, she wouldn't like animals. She wouldn't be unkind to them, just indifferent. In fact, thought Eliza, the girl wouldn't like anything which made a mess or needed looking after—not even children. Her home would be perfection itself, with not a cushion out of place and all the meals cooked to a high standard, and poor Christian would have no legitimate target for his bad temper, because that calm would never be shaken. They weren't suited, the pair of them. The thought struck her blindingly that not only did she love Christian more than anyone else in the world, but if she could bring it about, she would marry him herself.

'I wonder what you are thinking.' Professor van Duyl's voice was quiet, but she jumped all the same and said almost guiltily: 'Oh, nothing—nothing at all. Is the project here going well?'

'So far, yes. All ten men are showing a much greater resistance to asthmatic attacks—even Kok. I have discussed this problem of his mother-in-law every day and for the last two days there has been no single wheeze. It's not conclusive, of course, but I feel that we shall have proved that there is a way to tackle the problem, given time and more knowledge.'

Eliza poured them each more tea. 'Professor Wyllie has kept very well.'

'Yes, though I should warn you that when he gets an attack it is usually severe, and he is a very bad patient.'

'I should be too.' She remembered something. 'Do you suppose that I might have a half day or a morning off one day soon—just as long as it's before we go? I want to buy a present for Mrs MacRae.'

'You will drive yourself?' He sounded only politely interested. 'I don't see why not—arrangements can be made. Ullapool is the nearest shopping town; there is a road of sorts which joins the main road between Ledmore and Ullapool, it's narrow and has a poor surface, but I don't imagine that will deter you.'

Eliza didn't answer; she didn't relish the idea of driving the Fiat miles and miles along a difficult road, probably full of S-bends, gradients like the back stairs and fearful potholes, but she had no notion of letting him know that. Perhaps she could telephone and get something suitable sent out, but what? She had no idea, and Mrs MacRae, when delicately sounded, had been as informative as a clam. She would have to go to Ullapool and pray for fine weather.

There was no need for her prayers, however; two days later Professor Wyllie, pottering in to breakfast just as she was finishing hers in company with Doctor

Berrevoets and Doctor Peters, told her that young Grimshaw would keep an eye on the patients for the day and she was free to go to Ullapool as soon as she wished. 'But be back by teatime,' he begged her, 'so that you can take over for the usual evening duties.'

Eliza looked out of the window; Professor Wyllie had spoken with all the satisfied benevolence of one conferring a great treat, but it was hardly a day on which she would have chosen to go careering round unknown country in the little Fiat; the sky was grey and there was a light drizzle falling, and although the wind had moderated from gale force to a steady blow, it was unpleasant enough. With her unpleasant little adventure still fresh in her memory, she said doubtfully: 'Well, thank you, sir, but...'

'Christian has to go to Ullapool to collect some stuff we need, you can go with him.' He looked at his watch. 'He said to tell you in ten minutes' time at the front door.'

She said indignantly: 'But I'm going with the Fiat, he told me about the road—I...'

'He's changed his mind—and so have I. Eliza, this is no weather for you to go traipsing round on your own in that crackpot little car of yours.' He sounded quite testy.

'It brought me up from London,' she reminded him stubbornly.

'For which we are all deeply thankful. Go and get a coat on, child—you mustn't keep Christian waiting.'

She was tempted to dispute this high-handed remark,

but instead she excused herself nicely and made her way over to the cottage, where she reassured Cat, changed rapidly into a skirt and sweater, topped them with her matching tweed coat, tied a scarf over her hair, caught up handbag and gloves, and flew up to the Lodge, all within the space of the ten minutes allotted to her. She stopped by the kitchen as she went through the hall to ask Hub to keep an eye on Cat.

'Indeed I will, miss.' He was his usual paternal self. 'And I'll see that there's a nice fire burning, too—and is there anything else I can do?'

'No, thanks, Hub, you're an angel. Do you want anything from Ullapool?'

'Well, miss, me and Fred are partial to toffees, if you should have the time.'

'Of course. 'Bye for now.' She skipped through the hall, noticing as she went how nice the stairs looked now that they shone with polish, and out the front door. There was a Range Rover parked on the muddy sweep before the door with Christian behind its wheel. He got out when he saw her, wished her good morning and opened the car door for her to get in. As he settled himself beside her, she said with a trace of resentment: 'I could have quite well gone on my own.'

He was at his most bland. 'But of course—if the weather had been good.'

'But you told me—you even explained about the road.'

'Ah, yes.' The blandness had a silky note now. 'Do

you not feel, Eliza, that surprise when dealing with the enemy is of the utmost importance?'

If she hadn't loved him so much, she would have been furious, but all she felt was sadness that he was so determined not to like her. She agreed with him so soberly that he asked: 'Not sulking about it, I hope?'

Her voice was nicely composed. 'Of course not. I think I'm glad not to be going on my own. Is the road very awful?'

'Not too bad, and this goes anywhere.' He patted the wheel under his gloved hands as he drove down the track from the Lodge and on to the road which would lead them eventually to the main road to Ullapool.

Perhaps the bad road didn't seem so bad in the Range Rover; in the Fiat it would have been unspeakable. She sat contentedly beside him, looking at the different landmarks he pointed out as they went along. Even on such a dull grey morning as this was, the country was beautiful in a wild and grand fashion, and when they reached the road running beside Loch Lurgain, with Stac Polly towering on one side and the steel grey water on the other, she begged him to stop. 'I may never come this way again,' she pointed out, 'and it's quite breathtaking. Are there no villages at all?'

He shook his head. 'None. You could have come this way when you travelled up from London, you know, for it's quite a few miles further going round through Inchnadamph, even though it is a much better road. This one is lonely, especially after dark.'

They were standing together, watching the water. The wind was rustling through the rough grass and the bare trees, and made little waves on the loch. The drizzle had ceased now and the mountains on the other side of the water loomed forbiddingly. Eliza asked idly: 'Do you find it strange here? Isn't Holland flat?'

'Very, and of course it's hard to find an area as large as this where there is literally no one—the odd shepherd, I suppose, and foresters, but one seldom sees them.'

'Do you come here often?'

'I haven't been for several years. I came regularly at one time.'

'But it's so beautiful—and grand, too. You should bring your fiancée here.'

'She doesn't care for this type of country.' So that was why he didn't come any more. She sensed his withdrawal again and wondered about it. Surely it would have been natural enough for a man to talk about the girl he was going to marry, even if his listener wasn't amongst his friends—after all, they had worked together for three weeks now and although they quarrelled almost every time they met, they had a certain respect for each other's work. The idea that he didn't love Estelle returned with full force, but she pushed it resolutely to the back of her mind, and said lightly: 'I daresay I should dislike Holland.' She was thunderstruck when he said in a bitter voice: 'Because you dislike me, I suppose?' His mouth curled in a sneer. 'How illogical women are!'

'I am not…' she began, and then added lamely, 'It's so silly to quarrel.'

'Isn't bickering a better term? And since we seem unable to enjoy a pleasant conversation, we might as well go on.'

She fumed silently as he drove on; of all the unfair remarks, and she had only been trying to be friendly! Perhaps she had asked too many questions—well, that was easily remedied; she closed her pretty mouth firmly and stayed silent, an attitude which lost much of its value because he showed no disposition to talk anyway. It wasn't until they were approaching Ullapool that he said: 'My business will take about an hour. I suggest that we meet for coffee and then you can finish your shopping before lunch—there will be time for that before we need to go back.'

Eliza was still smarting from his unkind remarks. 'I should prefer to be on my own,' she told him haughtily. 'If you will tell me at what time we shall be returning I'll meet you then.'

Christian shrugged enormous shoulders. 'Just as you like.' His voice was annoyingly nonchalant. 'Three o'clock, then.'

They were in the main street by now and he drew up half way down it. 'Here,' he added, and scarcely looked at her as she got out. She walked away briskly, feeling hard done by, although she had to admit that it had been largely her fault; she could have had coffee with him at least. She took out her shopping list and studied it. She would find somewhere to have coffee, buy the small necessities on her list, and after lunch, look around for something suitable for Mrs MacRae. But the hotel she came upon was closed until the season started and she could see no café, so she gave up the idea of coffee, did her shopping and found her way easily enough to the shores of the loch. The water was still wild from the recent storms, the wind was blowing strongly still. Eliza enjoyed the exercise and felt her appetite sharpen. It prompted her to make for the centre of the town again; there must be a restaurant somewhere where she could get a meal; the hotels she had passed on her walk were all closed, but probably she hadn't explored enough. She was on the point of crossing the road to turn into the main street once more when she became aware of the man standing beside her.

'And what's a pretty little girl like you doing in this godforsaken hole?'

The voice was jovial, but the face, when she looked at it in some surprise, was thin and ratlike, and she disliked the smile. She didn't bother to answer him, but crossed the road, only to have him cross it with her and lay a hand on her arm as they reached the other side. 'What about a meal, girlie?'

She frowned at being called girlie. 'I don't know you,' she told him icily, 'and I don't want to. Kindly leave me alone.' She made to pass him, but his hand tightened. 'Not so fast, my dear...' He winced as she kicked him smartly on the shin and then burst into a roar of laughter.

'You little vixen,' he declared. 'I like a bit of spirit.'

There was no one in sight at all; just round the corner there were shops and people, but here, on the deserted road by the loch, there was no one. Which made it all the more remarkable that Christian should be suddenly there, between them. The rat-faced man was pushed away with one hand, while Eliza felt the other catch her comfortably round the waist.

'Get out,' said the Professor very quietly, 'and fast. I am a man of violent temper.' He didn't bother to watch the man turn and hurry away, but took his arm from Eliza's waist and tucked it under her arm and walked her away too, in the opposite direction.

'You see what comes of being pig-headed?' he demanded of her in a furious voice. 'Miss High-and-Mighty has to go off on her own and sulk. You deserve the unwelcome attentions of all the rat-faced commercial travellers you meet!'

Eliza had been buoyed up by indignation, fright and then the sudden relief and delight at Christian's opportune arrival, but now the desire to have a good cry had overcome those feelings. She trotted along beside her irate companion, who was walking much too fast for her, and the tears rolled silently down her cheeks. Perhaps it was the fact that she hadn't made her usual spirited rejoinder to any remark of his which made him glance down at her. He stopped so suddenly that she almost fell over, and swung her round to face him, his hands on her shoulders.

'Eliza,' and he sounded quite shocked, 'my dear girl, you're crying!'

She found her voice. 'Well, so would you if you were me.' She sniffed. 'You're quite beastly—anyone would think that I went out looking for r-rat-faced men, and all I wanted was my d-dinner.'

He made a small sound which might have been a laugh. 'Eliza, I'm sorry—I was worse than the rat-faced man, wasn't I? I think I was angry and didn't stop to think what I was saying.'

He wiped her tears away in a kindly, detached way and said: 'Better now? There's a small inn along here where we can get a meal, come along.'

It was close by, a whitewashed, low-built pub, very neat as to windows, its solid door freshly painted. Eliza, who would have liked to have finished her crying in peace, found herself ushered into its bar and then out of it again into the snuggery at the back, where there was a brisk fire burning and a small table covered with a checked tablecloth and laid for a meal. The Professor came to a halt in this comfortable apartment, unbuttoned her coat and took it from her and offered her a seat by the fire.

'Stay there,' he told her. 'I'll be back.'

He was as good as his word; she barely had the time to peer at her tear-stained face in her compact mirror before he was back again with two glasses. He handed one to her. 'Brandy,' he offered, 'it will do you good.'

'I never drink brandy.'

'I should hope not. But this is a medicinal dose, ordered by a doctor, so drink up.'

It would be useless to argue, so Eliza drank and felt its warmth at once; it also gave her the feeling that life wasn't so bad after all, and when Christian suggested that she might like to go and tidy her hair and do her face, she agreed quite meekly, and when she got back, very neat about the head and with a slightly heightened colour, the landlord was at the table with a loaded tray, and instead of going back to the fire she was invited to sit at table. She took her place opposite her companion, smiling a little uncertainly at him.

'Is it convenient?—for me to have lunch here, I mean. It doesn't look as though they…'

'I telephoned this morning before we left. There's nothing much open during the winter here, but this place will always give us lunch if we warn them.'

'Oh, I'm eating yours, then.'

'You're eating your own, Eliza. I ordered for both of us.'

She had no answer but to drink her soup, glad of something to do. It was delicious, as was the fish which followed it. By the time they had reached the mouthwatering steamed pudding set before them, she was relaxed enough to reply to his easy talk of this and that, and the Riesling they were drinking, continuing the good work the brandy had begun, made her feel quite her old self, sufficiently so, indeed, to allow her to thank him for coming to her aid. 'That's three times,' she pointed out seriously, 'if you don't count Cat. I've been rather a nuisance to you.'

He didn't answer but asked her instead if he might accompany her in her search for a present for Mrs MacRae. Eliza accepted happily; he might disapprove of her, but just now and again he seemed to forget that he didn't like her and they were like old friends.

She found what she wanted for Mrs MacRae, a quilted dressing gown in a cheerful pink. 'For,' she pointed out matter-of-factly to the Professor, 'it's no good buying her tweed or woollies—I mean, coals to Newcastle, isn't it? although there are some lovely things in that handicrafts shop across the street, but they make them in her village, don't they?' She nodded her pretty head at him. 'She needs something impractical because she's such a practical person, you see. I thought I'd get her the largest box of chocolates I can find.'

But here her companion had something to say. 'May I suggest that I send down to London and get a really glamorous box?'

'Oh, lovely—embossed velvet and ribbons and

simply enormous and quite quite useless, she'll love it. That would be simply marvellous.'

She didn't see him smile as they crossed the road to examine the contents of the handicrafts shop window. 'You like these tweeds?' he wanted to know.

She nodded. 'They're heavenly—look at that red one—like holly, and that green checked one on the corner. You should buy some for your fiancée, you only need a yard for a skirt.'

She was sorry immediately she had spoken, for he said in a cold voice: 'Estelle doesn't care for tweed. She has an excellent and sophisticated taste in clothes.'

Eliza cast an involuntary glance at her own small person, so sensibly tweed-clad. There was nothing sophisticated about her, she was afraid. She glanced up and met the Professor's eye and lifted her chin at the intentness of his look; probably he was comparing her with his precious Estelle. 'I must find a sweet shop,' she said abruptly. 'I promised that I'd buy Hub and Fred some toffees.'

He gave a rumble of laughter. 'I'm surprised you didn't come armed with a list of odds and ends from the patients too. Here's a shop, let us buy these toffees and make for home. I believe the weather is breaking up again.'

'But it's been raining on and off all day,' she pointed out.

'Oh, rain—that's to be expected. But the wind's rising.'

He was right; by the time they had reached the road

by the loch the gale was upon them, beating round the Range Rover, sweeping the rain in torrents against the windscreen. Eliza, profoundly thankful that she wasn't driving the Fiat, sat quietly beside Christian, who didn't seem to mind the weather in the least, although keeping the car on the narrow road was a task she didn't envy him. Once or twice she was tempted to beg him to stop and wait until the worst was over, but it would be dark soon. Besides, he might think that she was frightened, and she wasn't—not with him, so she clenched her teeth tightly and made no sound, not even when the car lurched into a deeper pothole than most and she thought they were stuck. But they weren't. Christian, muttering darkly in his own language, reversed, then roared forward into the rain-sodden gloom.

Hardly an enjoyable trip, Eliza thought as he brought the car to a halt at the Lodge front door, and yet it had been wonderful; she had been with him for hours and even if she hadn't been sure before, she knew now that there wasn't another man like him—not for her, anyway.

The sweep was a sea of muddy water once more; he came round the bonnet and opened her door and lifted her out to dump her gently in the porch.

'Go down to the cottage through the house,' he advised her. 'I'll bring the parcels.'

She did as she was told and found the little place warm and lighted and a tea tray laid ready. Cat sat up, purring loudly as she went in, and she paused only long enough to take off her coat before fetching a saucer of milk. She would put the kettle on, she told Cat, and when Christian came they would have a cup of tea; there were little cakes on the tray and she would make some buttered toast, he would be hungry… But when he came, five minutes later, he gave her a bleak refusal when she suggested it, only putting the parcels on the table for her, and pausing briefly to speak to Cat and the kittens. At the door he halted, though, when Eliza said in a level little voice, 'Thank you for my lunch and for driving me, Professor. It was a lovely day.'

He turned right round and looked at her frowningly. She still had her headscarf on; it was wet and bedraggled and there were a number of damp curls hanging untidily round her face, which no longer showed any signs of make-up. He said almost angrily, 'A lovely day,' and then, as though the words were being dragged out of him, 'And a lovely girl.'

CHAPTER SIX

ELIZA drank her tea thoughtfully. She wasn't a con-
ceited girl, but the Professor's words, wrung from him,
she felt sure, most unwillingly, had given her food for
contemplation; she was well aware that she was a very
pretty girl and that men reacted quite naturally to this,
but the Professor wasn't quite the same as most of the
men she knew; for one thing he was engaged to be
married, and for another, he hadn't shown any signs of
liking her when they had met. Indeed, she wasn't certain
that he liked her even now, although she was aware that
she had made an impression upon him, reluctantly
received on his part. She poured more tea and fell to
thinking about Estelle. It was perhaps a little unsport-
ing to try and take him away from the highly bred,
slightly bored girl in the photograph, but Eliza was quite
sure that Estelle wasn't the right girl for him. She
wondered if he had discovered that for himself by now.
Men, she thought bitterly, could be so very blind, but it

was no good wasting time on speculation. There was only a little over a week left before she would return to St Anne's, not very long a time in which to capture a man's attention and his heart as well, but at least she would have a good try.

She tidied away the tea things and changed into uniform, talking to Cat while she did so, and then, well wrapped against the weather, went over to the hut. It was disappointing that she didn't see Professor van Duyl again that evening.

Indeed, she hardly saw him at all during the next few days. True, he came down to the hut when a patient showed signs of starting an attack, and on routine visits, but Eliza was never alone with him. She suspected him of contriving that, and it could only mean one of two things; either he disliked her so much that he avoided her at all costs, or he realized the danger in getting to know her better. She liked to think it was the second reason, and despite the shortness of the time left to her, took heart, especially as a short conversation she had with him at the lunch table confirmed her suspicions about his feelings for his fiancée.

They had been discussing the breaking up of the scheme, now five days away, and she had brought up, rather anxiously, the question of Cat. 'I think I shall take her with me,' she told Professor Wyllie. 'She and the kittens can travel in the car and I'll have to put them into a cats' home near the hospital until I go home.'

The old man smiled at her. 'Your parents won't object to three pets?'

She hesitated. 'Well, perhaps at first. I'll try and find good homes for Primus and Secundus as soon as I can.'

'Supposing I were to take them to my home?' suggested Professor van Duyl suddenly. 'They will be company for the kitchen cat as well as my own.'

Eliza turned to him impulsively. 'Oh, that would be nice, they could all live together then.' She remembered something. 'But it wouldn't do—you said that—that you didn't want any more animals.'

'I'? His look was bland. He drank the rest of his coffee and sat back in his chair as people began to leave the table and when she made to get up too: 'No, you are off duty, are you not, therefore in no hurry for a few moments. Why did you say that?'

'Well, you did say only a little while ago that you weren't going to have any more animals at your home because your fiancée didn't much care for them. Besides, three cats—and you've got three cats and a dog already, you might not have room, and they'll cost quite a lot to feed.'

A curious expression passed over his face. 'Oh, I think I can fit them in, and I must persuade Estelle to accept them. After all, we shall not marry for a month or two; Cat and her kittens will have had time to learn their way around the house.'

Eliza felt doubtful. 'Yes, but you see, if your fiancée

doesn't like them, she might want them to live outside. You have got a garden?' she added anxiously.

He smiled a little. 'Oh, yes. But I will take care to see that that doesn't happen.' He went on with a sudden fierceness: 'I have the impression that you are prepared to dislike Estelle, Sister Proudfoot. I must remind you that she is a well-balanced and intelligent young woman, not in the least impulsive, and I have never known her deviate from her own very high standards of conduct.'

'She sounds like a crushing bore,' said Eliza before she could stop herself and then gasped: 'Oh, Christian, I'm sorry! I—I never meant…'

He had gone a little white around his mouth and his eyes were so dark that they might have been black. 'How dare you? And I beg of you, make no excuses. I have no idea why you should make such a vulgar remark about someone of whom you know nothing.' He got up and went and stood by the still smouldering fire, his back towards her. 'And you of all people,' he went on, more fiercely than ever, 'an impulsive, aggravating young woman who should know better.'

Eliza had got to her feet too. She said in a tight voice, 'I'm not making excuses, I can merely repeat that I'm sorry and very ashamed of myself.' At the door she couldn't resist adding: 'That should make you feel very happy.'

And later, at the end of the day, when she was back in her cottage after an afternoon and evening of avoiding Christian at all costs, she remembered, as she undressed in a storm of angry tears, that she had called him Christian. 'I'm an utter fool,' she told Cat, 'a jealous, meddlesome fool. I deserve his contempt and now I've got it.'

Cat yawned cosily, made a small comforting sound and curled up round her kittens. 'I shall miss you,' Eliza told her as she put out the light, 'but it's nice to think of you with him—and he did say he'd take care of you, so he will.' She lay awake for a long time, trying to imagine what his home was like; comfortable for certain, for he was a successful man in his profession. He dressed well and his clothes were superbly cut and she was sure that his shirts were of silk. Her thoughts sidetracked; how did he manage to present such a pristine appearance to the world with no laundry in sight; had he paid Mrs MacRae extravagant sums to press his trousers and iron his shirts, or perhaps he did them himself? The idea was so absurd that she giggled rather forlornly and at last went to sleep.

The remaining days passed all too quickly, and then it was the last day and the farewell tea-party for Mrs MacRae. Fred had excelled himself with the making of an iced cake, and Christian, true to his word, presented her with one of the largest, most extravagant boxes of chocolates Eliza had ever seen, and as well as that a bulky envelope the contents of which she guessed was money. Her own gift she had already given, and when she had seen Mrs MacRae's plain face light up as she had unwrapped it, she was glad that she had chosen something so pink and pretty. 'It'll wash and dry like a rag,' she told Mrs MacRae, 'so you can wear it every day if you want to.'

Mrs MacRae's 'Aye,' was ecstatic.

And Eliza herself had had an unexpected present too—from the patients; a small painting, done by a local artist, showing the Lodge and the surrounding countryside. 'So that you will not forget us,' Mijnheer Kok, voted spokesman, had said with such sincerity that the tears had pricked her eyelids.

But now all that was over and they were on their way; the Range Rover in front with the four doctors, herself following in the Fiat and Hub driving a minibus with the patients and the remainder of the staff. They were to spend the night in Edinburgh, some two hundred and fifty miles away, and luckily the weather had cleared so that this time, in early daylight and with someone ahead to guide her, Eliza enjoyed the journey.

She had decided on a policy of avoiding Christian, which was perhaps a little pointless, for he was quite obviously doing the same, but it was the only way of finding out if he had any interest in her at all. She stayed with the patients when they stopped on the road for meals, and that evening at the hotel she joined them at dinner too, leaving the occupants of the Rover to share a table and entertain themselves, something which they did rather successfully, she reflected, listening to the gusts of laughter. She told Cat about it as she got ready for bed in the pleasant room at the hotel, for Cat, after being fed and suitably dealt with by Hub, had been delegated to her for the night. She sat in her box, quite unworried by the excitements of the journey, the kittens curled close to her, and watched Eliza with her round eyes, making gentle little sounds by way of answer.

'Do you suppose I'm barking up the wrong tree, Cat?' Eliza demanded as she got into bed, but all Cat did was to purr.

The Dutch contingent parted from them in the morning, to fly to Holland under the rather absent-minded guardianship of Doctor Berrevoets. Eliza, shaking them each by the hand and wishing them goodbye, hoped fervently that none of them would begin to wheeze, for she very much doubted if he knew what would be expected of him, although she had seen Christian in earnest conversation with him before they left. The remainder of the party pushed on to Nottingham, and Eliza, eating her dinner with the five English patients who were left, brooded on the fact that she and Professor van Duyl hadn't spoken to each other for the entire day, beyond a chilly good morning and such social niceties as offering cups of tea and passing the salt. And the next day was the last on which she would see him, for half way between Northampton and Luton they would part company, she to travel on to London, the rest of them to go their various ways and the two professors to go across country to the small village near Halstead where Professor Wyllie lived. Presumably Christian would go back to his home from there; if she had been on better terms with him she might have asked, and she didn't like to bother Professor Wyllie who was looking tired and ill, although he had refused to admit that he was either when she taxed him with it. Eliza wished him goodbye after breakfast and he made her a nice little speech before she went to find everyone else and wish them goodbye too. She would miss Hub; she lingered with him, talking about Cat rather wistfully, putting off the moment when she would have to bid goodbye to Christian. She had failed dismally and she had been quite wrong; he didn't care a cent for her—worse, he was indifferent. She shook Hub's hand, tickled Cat under her now plump chin, and turned to go.

'The Professor is in the coffee room,' Hub said quietly. 'He came looking for you, miss, but you were with the men. He was afraid of missing you and asked me to mention it—indeed, he said I was to be sure and tell you.'

She thanked him in a voice which didn't quite conceal her feelings and went back to the hotel. She hadn't noticed the coffee room when they had arrived the night before, but it didn't matter, as it turned out, for Christian was waiting for her. 'In here, Sister Proudfoot,' he invited, and held the door wide.

He shut it firmly behind her and said without preamble: 'We have been avoiding each other.'

'Yes. You wanted that, didn't you?'

His dark eyes gleamed at that, but she didn't see because for some reason he had put on his glasses. But his next remark surprised her.

'No, I didn't want it, Eliza.' He sighed in an exasperated sort of way. 'My dear good girl, you must know that you are a very attractive woman—I find you more than that; an amusing companion, kind and thoughtful, high-spirited, tender-hearted—absurdly so—fiercely independent and yet needing to be taken care of.' He frowned fiercely at her. 'In fact, you have disrupted my calm life. I am thankful that after today we shan't meet again. You have caused enough havoc.'

She wondered, in a detached way, what he would say if she told him that she hadn't really tried…now, if she had made up her mind the moment she had first met him and had had the whole four weeks… She said coldly: 'You make yourself very plain, but I must point out that if you loved your fiancée you wouldn't have even noticed me, and as for disrupting your life I've done no such thing—and you said it, not I. Anyway, you'll forget me the moment I'm out of sight.'

There was a good deal she would have liked to have said, but suddenly the tears crowded into her throat, making it impossible. She walked to the door, but he got there first.

'You're wrong,' he sounded goaded. 'I'll not forget you, Eliza,' and kissed her with a ferocity which took her breath, opened the door and pushed her into the foyer. She heard the door close behind her, but she didn't look round. The Fiat was outside, there was nothing to keep her any longer. Eliza got in, waved unseeingly at the little group standing by the bus, and drove away.

Her mind was a numb thing for the first ten miles or so. She went steadily down the M1, not thinking at all, but presently the numbness wore off, leaving pain and bewilderment. Christian had said that he was thankful that he would never see her again, and yet he had kissed her like a man who wanted to see her again very much. Her head began to ache with all the might-have-beens, and even while she told herself it was useless to dwell on regrets, they crept back into her mind, popping out to plague her.

She was no distance from London now and there seemed no point in getting to St Anne's too early in the afternoon. She turned off the motorway at St Albans and had lunch—a waste of money, as it turned out, for she had no appetite, but it had whiled away an hour, and since she still had time to spare she didn't go back to the motorway, but took a secondary road into London, taking her time now so that it was five o'clock by the time she had put the car away, taken her case up to her room and had a cup of tea, and that finished she tidied herself without much interest and went down to the Office. Miss Smythe would want to see her, she supposed; besides, there was the question of days off.

She had had none at all at Inverpolly, and she hadn't bothered about them, but now there were eight days to come to her. She would go home, she decided as she made her way through the hospital, then come back and get down to work. It looked as though she was going to be a career girl after all.

She found Miss Smythe still on duty and looking as near agitated as such a dignified being could permit. She wasted very little time on returning Eliza's polite greeting, but exclaimed: 'How fortunate, Sister Proudfoot, that you should come at this very moment. I have just this minute received an urgent telephone call from Professor Wyllie's house. He has been taken ill—heart, as you know, and a nasty turn of asthma. He asks that you should go there immediately and look after him until he has recovered.' She looked at Eliza with a certain smugness. 'He thinks very highly of you.'

Eliza stared at her, hardly believing her ears. 'But, Miss Smythe, I've only just arrived—I've not unpacked…'

Miss Smythe didn't seem to have heard her. 'An hour?' she enquired smoothly. 'Is that long enough for you to get some things together, Sister? Someone called—er—Hub is coming to fetch you.'

'But I don't know where Professor Wyllie lives. Besides, I…'

She was ruthlessly cut short. 'North Essex, or is it Suffolk, I'm not certain, but what does it matter?' Miss

Smythe dismissed the geographical details with a commanding wave of the hand.

'I've eight days off due to me,' Eliza stated, feeling as hopeless as a bridge player with no trumps.

Miss Smythe tutted. 'Men,' she observed succinctly, 'so thoughtless—so unable to cope.'

Eliza remembered her unfortunate experience in the gale and the mist; Christian had coped very nicely then, as he had with Cat and the flooded cottage—even the rat-faced man.

'Well, Sister?' Miss Smythe's voice was brisk and brought her back to the present with a rush.

'Very well,' Eliza said meekly, 'though I can't think why Professor Wyllie should want me there.'

'You are a good nurse,' her superior smiled with brief kindness. 'You have the gift of never allowing your patients to doubt that they will recover. They like that.'

Eliza was ready by six o'clock; she had even had time to go along to Men's Medical and talk to Mary Price, who managed to give her a potted resumé of the month's happenings together with news of staff changes, a new houseman, and the added information that she was going steady with the Surgical Registrar. Eliza made appropriate replies, expressed delight at Mary's matrimonial prospects, gave a brief report of her own life at Inverpolly, and raced back to her room to get her newly packed case.

Hub was waiting for her in the Range Rover, which

somehow looked out of place in the heart of London, but she accorded it the briefest of attention. 'I never expected to see you again, Hub,' she exclaimed as she climbed in beside him. 'You must tell me what's happened.' She turned to smile at him.

He smiled back at her and manoeuvred the car out of the forecourt into the busy street.

'Professor Wyllie didn't feel very well—you noticed, didn't you, miss? He had a bad turn just after we got to his home. Luckily I had dropped the last of the others off at Cambridge and got back very soon after the two professors. I was sent at once to fetch you—if you would come.'

'You mean Professor Wyllie sent for me?'

'He asked for you, miss.'

So Christian had gone; presumably Hub would go back to Holland to wherever he lived as soon as he had delivered her safely.

He drove well, making light of the snarled-up city traffic, and once clear of it, driving fast. Christian drove fast, too, she remembered wistfully, and buried the thought. 'You know the way,' she commented after a while.

'Yes, miss—I've been this way several times.'

He had avoided the busy Chelmsford road and had gone through Fyfield and Great Bardfield and turned off there for Sible Hedingham, to turn off once more into a narrow country lane, its low hedges picked out by the Range Rover's powerful lights. There was nothing to see in the dark, and presently Eliza said: 'A bit lonely isn't it?'

'Yes, miss—there's the church and some houses round the next bend, Professor Wyllie's house is just beyond them. Very nice it is too in the summer.'

She wanted to ask him how it was he knew so much about the old professor's home, but didn't like to; she wasn't quite sure who he was to begin with and although he had always answered her questions he had never volunteered any information about himself. 'You do live in Holland, don't you?' she ventured.

'Oh, yes, miss. Here is the village.'

They swept round a small village green with the dim outlines of the houses surrounding it, and on past the church before turning in through an open white-painted gate, to pull up before the door through whose transom light was streaming.

The door was opened by Miss Trim, looking worried. She said: 'How do you do, Miss Proudfoot. I hope you're not too inconvenienced by this,' because she was the sort of person who would consider it unthinkable not to observe the civilities of everyday life however trying the circumstances. And when Eliza murmured suitably: 'I'm Miss Trim, Professor Wyllie's secretary. I live in the village, but it seemed right that I should remain here until you arrived.' Her eyes focused over Eliza's shoulder. 'Hub, would you be so kind as to take me home?'

He put Eliza's case down in the lobby. 'Of course, Miss Trim. Shall I just let someone know that Sister Proudfoot is here?'

'I'll do that and fetch my coat at the same time.' She turned to Eliza. 'If you would come with me? There's a housekeeper here—she has prepared a room and has a meal ready. She's a very competent woman.'

They crossed the square hall together and Eliza asked: 'How is the professor?'

'Rather poorly, I'm afraid. The doctor came a short time ago and consulted… In here.'

She opened the door at the back of the hall as she spoke and ushered Eliza inside. The room was pleasantly warm, large and well lighted. There was a large, untidy desk at one end of it and Christian was sitting at it. Eliza heard Miss Trim wish them both good night before she went away, closing the door quietly behind her.

Eliza found her breath and said the first thing to enter her whirling head. 'Oh, hullo—how very awkward, meeting like this again. A—a kind of anticlimax.'

He had got up from his chair. 'I don't think I should call it that,' he answered quietly. He seemed larger than ever, standing there. Perhaps he had grown since she had seen him last, she thought absurdly. She shut her eyes and opened them again because she felt peculiar, and found him beside her. 'You're tired and hungry,' he stated in the kind, detached voice of his profession. 'Sit down.' He pushed her gently into a chair and went to a cupboard in the wall and came back with a glass in his hand.

'Professor Wyllie wants to see you, otherwise I'd

send you straight to bed. Drink this; it will get you up the stairs at least. Presently you shall have a meal.'

Eliza sipped and her head cleared a little. She got up carefully. 'I'm quite all right now. Is Professor Wyllie very ill?'

They were walking to the door and she hardly noticed his hand under her elbow. 'Yes, but he'll pull through, especially if he has you to look after him.'

They went upstairs and into a large room filled with heavy furniture. The old man was sitting up in bed, propped against a great many pillows, his eyes closed. Eliza had never seen him look like that before, tired to death and not bothering any more, but as she looked at him he opened his eyes and winked at her.

'Good girl,' he managed. 'Knew you'd come. Now I'll do.'

She went over to the bed and took his hand. 'Of course you'll do,' she told him hearteningly. 'Now go to sleep, there's a dear.'

They waited while he dropped off again and then went back downstairs where Christian handed her over to Mrs Moore, the housekeeper, a small, round woman who looked upset and excited as well. 'You come with me, Sister,' she breathed in a hushed voice, 'I've a nice hot supper for you.'

Professor van Duyl turned away. 'I'll be in the study when you're ready.' He spoke carelessly, already crossing the hall, away from her.

Eliza ate her supper, too tired to know what she was eating, listening to Mrs Moore's hushed voice recounting the dramatic events of the evening, and longing for her bed. But it was more than likely that she would be expected to sit with Professor Wyllie—someone would have to be there; Mrs Moore, though a nice woman, was obviously useless from a nursing point of view and there didn't seem to be any one else around but Christian and Hub, and he had gone down to the village. Eliza drank the last of the coffee and went back to the study, to receive explicit details of the patient from his colleague and instructions to go to bed at once, so that she might get up at four o'clock the next morning and take over the care of the patient.

'Yes, but who's to look after him during the night?' she wanted to know.

'I shall. Before you go we will run over the treatment…'

She sat down beside him and went carefully through the notes on the desk; the treatment and the drugs and the possibilities of things going wrong. 'A pity he can't tolerate the cortisones,' remarked the Professor. 'His heart condition rules that out—neither dare we use atrophine. He's on aminophyline injections at present—Doctor Trent, the local GP, agrees with me that they will be the most helpful in this case. Diuretics and a low salt diet, of course. I gave him morphine, as you see in the notes, very soon after the attack started. It should carry him through the greater part of the night and by the time you come on duty we can re-assess his condition.'

Eliza got to her feet, swallowed a yawn and in a voice which she strove to make unconcerned, asked: 'Are you staying until Professor Wyllie is better?'

'I had intended to return to Holland tonight; I shall stay for another twenty-four hours, longer if there is any need, but I have certain commitments…' he paused. 'Doctor Trent is a very good man.' He got up too and came round the desk. 'Rest assured, Eliza, that I shan't go if I'm needed here—Professor Wyllie and I are very old friends.' He opened the door for her. 'Mrs Moore will show you your room—have you an alarm clock with you?'

'Yes, thank you. Good night, sir.'

'You called me Christian.' His voice was faintly amused, and because she didn't know what to answer she said nothing at all, but crossed the hall to where Mrs Moore, very much on the alert, was waiting for her.

Her room was pleasant enough, although rather over furnished with mid-Victorian furniture, but the bed was a splendid one and Mrs Moore had warmed it thoroughly. Eliza undressed rapidly, had a quick bath and curled up in its comfort.

It seemed a bare ten minutes before the alarm went off. She dressed in the dazed, disciplined way night nurses quickly learn, put up her hair into an uncaring bun, left her face without make-up, and crept along the landing to her patient's room, looking, did she but know it, like a small girl dressed up in a nurse's uniform. Perhaps the same idea crossed Professor van Duyl's mind as she went in, for he got out of his chair with the hint of a smile. But there was nothing childlike about her manner. Eliza took his report with grave attention, asked a couple of pertinent questions, made sure that she knew where she could lay hands on the drugs and syringes should she need them urgently, checked the patient's pulse as he lay sleeping, agreed to waken Christian should she deem it necessary, and prepared to take up her duty.

'There's tea in the thermos,' said the Professor from the door. 'I'll be back to relieve you for breakfast.'

'That won't be necessary,' she said at once. 'I can have some coffee or something when I get Professor Wyllie whatever he wants.'

'I'm quite sure you can, nevertheless I shall be here to relieve you for breakfast. Good night.'

Her patient wakened two hours later, declaring himself to be quite recovered and promptly began to wheeze. 'Now, now,' said Eliza in a motherly voice, 'that's enough of that,' and had him propped up and an injection given before he had a chance to argue, then waited quietly until the wheezing had died down before she began to ready her patient for the day. 'Like a cup of tea?' she asked as she charted his TPR.

'What is the time, girl? Could we not have a cup together?'

'Of course—I'll go and get it, and don't you dare move until I get back.'

He grinned tiredly at her, but he wasn't looking so exhausted now; provided that he rested for a few days, he would be his own self again; not quite as fit as before, perhaps, but able to resume his usual life. He wasn't a man to take kindly to invalidism and the fact that he would have to slow down a little because of his heart wouldn't prevent him doing exactly what he wanted. He was a stubborn man, but Eliza rather liked him for that as well as admiring his courage; not many men of his age and in his condition would have risked going into the wilds of Scotland, miles from a hospital—though he'd had Christian, she conceded as she put on the kettle and assembled a tea tray; if she had been in like case and Christian had been there, however remote the spot, she would have felt quite safe too.

The Professor arrived at exactly half past eight, looking, as he had done once before, wide awake, well fed and immaculate. Eliza wondered how he did it and catching sight of her own reflection in the vast mirror of the dressing table, deplored her own rather hagged appearance. No make-up, she moaned silently, and hair in wisps, but her tired face, even without make-up, was still delightfully pretty, and hair in wisps, when it curled, didn't matter at all. Christian gave her a long, keen look as he came in and she frowned back at him because it could only mean that he found her just as untidy as she felt, but she forgot that instantly because there was the brief report to give him before she went down to breakfast.

'And after breakfast,' he said, seeing her to the door, 'you will go for a brisk walk, and be good enough to return here at eleven o'clock.'

She opened her mouth to argue this point, but he said swiftly: 'No, don't, it's such a waste of time,' and flashed her a sudden smile which transformed him from a severe-faced doctor into a delightful man whom she loved desperately.

She not only went for a brisk walk after a substantial breakfast, she had a bath, did her face with great care, her hair as well, and presented herself, as fresh as the proverbial daisy, at exactly eleven o'clock. Her patient was asleep.

'We'll leave him,' counselled the Professor. 'He needs a good rest. See that he has a light meal when he wakes and keep him as quiet as possible—he's pulled round nicely. Given a week of taking things easy he should be almost as good as new.'

'No need to keep him in bed?'

He shook his head. 'Not after the next day or so, but you will have to be firm with him, he can be stubborn. I don't imagine that he will have another attack, but use the oxygen if you need to and I've written up his drugs. Get him out of bed for half an hour if he feels like it.' He strolled away. 'I'll be around if you want me and Doctor Trent will be calling this afternoon.'

Time crawled by. Professor Wyllie slept, opened his eyes to take stock of her, smiled, and slept again. Just after two o'clock he wakened properly, demanded to get out of bed, eat his lunch and put through a few telephone calls.

Eliza dealt with him firmly. 'Lunch first,' she told him, 'then you may get up for half an hour exactly. The telephoning can wait until Doctor Trent has seen you.'

'Monster!' declared her patient. 'No one would think, looking at you…'

'It's a great asset and the secret of my success,' she told him lightly, and went downstairs to get his lunch tray.

Mrs Moore was in the kitchen and a tray was ready on the table with soup heating on the stove and an egg custard ready on its dish. She made haste to pour coffee for Eliza the moment she opened the kitchen door with a sympathetic: 'You poor thing, you've not had a bite to eat.'

'That's OK, but the coffee's lovely,' said Eliza gratefully. 'Oh, you've got Cat here.'

'That's right, Hub brought them here while he packs up, he and Professor van Duyl are going this afternoon. He thought the little creatures would be better here under my eye, no chance of getting scared or trying to run away.'

Eliza took the tray upstairs, her thoughts busy. Christian had mentioned that he might be leaving today, but she hadn't really believed him because she hadn't wanted to, but now it seemed likely that she wouldn't see him again; there was no sign of him around the house; he had forgotten about her lunch—perhaps he had already gone. And Hub? He hadn't gone yet. Were they travelling together? she wondered. She wasn't sure about Hub; she supposed he was someone the professor knew well. Perhaps he worked in a hospital, so they would probably join forces for the journey? By plane? By boat? She had no idea, and no time to indulge in speculation.

She stood over Professor Wyllie while he ate his lunch, got him out of bed with care, sat him in a large, high-backed chair and made his bed for him, all the while talking gently about nothing much so that he wouldn't sit and think about himself. She was on the point of getting him back into bed again when the door opened and Christian and a youngish man whom she took to be Doctor Trent came in, both to become immediately absorbed in their older colleague. It was ten minutes or more before they had concluded their examination, greatly hindered by their patient's forcefully expressed opinions.

'You're on the mend, sir,' pronounced Christian, 'but you must rest for several days—Sister Proudfoot will see to that.'

'She's a tartar,' muttered Professor Wyllie, and chuckled at her, standing like a statue at the foot of his bed. All three gentlemen looked at her, Doctor Trent in open admiration, her patient with an air of mischief, and Professor van Duyl with no expression on his handsome face at all.

She looked back at them, her eyebrows slightly raised. 'Shall I come back presently, sir?' she asked.

The old man chuckled again. 'Not much of you,' he commented weakly, 'but what there is is good sound stuff. You stay here, girl, and give us a chance to stare at you; we don't often get the chance of seeing such a pretty girl.'

Eliza accepted this speech with composure. 'You've been out of bed a great deal longer than half an hour,' she pointed out, and proceeded to pop him back into bed, helped by Doctor Trent.

Professor van Duyl didn't lift a finger, merely enquired: 'He ate his lunch, Sister?'

'Every crumb.' Perhaps it was something in her voice which made him look sharply at her. 'Your own lunch—I had entirely overlooked it—you've had none.'

She agreed with him, feeling suddenly hollow. 'But don't worry,' she begged him, 'Mrs. Moore gave me a cup of coffee when I went down for the tray.'

'You'll go now, please. I shall remain here until you return—is half an hour sufficient? I am very sorry; I had a number of calls to make to Holland…'

She forgave him with a smile. Estelle, of course, whether he loved her or not. Presumably he would go and see her the moment he got back home. She ran downstairs, her head full of unhappy little pictures of the two of them meeting once more, and perhaps she had been mistaken after all and Estelle wasn't in the least like her photograph. Perhaps, just for Christian, she would come alive and warm and loving, perhaps she herself had allowed her imagination to run away with her because she had so wanted him to fall in love with her—and he hadn't.

She ate a hurried meal with Mrs Moore fussing round her, then went back on duty to find the doctors ready to leave. Doctor Trent wished her goodbye in a friendly fashion and said he would be back again in the morning and that she was to call him if she was worried. Christian wished her goodbye too, so casually that she barely murmured in reply, not realizing that this really was goodbye, for when she went down to get Professor Wyllie his tea, it was to hear he and Hub had gone and Cat and her kittens with them. Mrs Moore, a little curious, gave her a note from Hub, regretting not having seen her to wish her goodbye and promising that he would take good care of Cat and her offspring. Eliza read it twice as though there might be something in it she had missed, then took the tray upstairs, feeling lost.

She went through the rest of the day like a well-trained automaton, not believing that Christian could have gone away like that with no more than a careless word. It was a good thing that as the hours passed, her patient gathered strength and became quite irascible, making peppery remarks which she knew he didn't mean and requiring a good deal of soothing before she could settle him for the night and give him his sleeping pill, sitting prudently by his bed until she was quite sure that he was sound asleep, before going to her own room, where, unlike her patient, she didn't sleep a wink.

CHAPTER SEVEN

ELIZA had given the Professor his breakfast the next morning, and had her own, when she decided to take a quick walk around the garden before going back to her patient. Snuggled into her cape, she went out of the front door and round the side of the house to the sizeable garden at the back, stopping to peep in the garage as she passed it. The Fiat was there; she stood and stared at it in amazement, then hurried back to the kitchen. 'Mrs Moore,' she asked, 'do you know how my car got here?'

'Why, bless you, Sister, Professor van Duyl asked Hub to go for it yesterday—didn't he tell you?' She shook her head. 'Forgetful, that's what he is, forgot your nice hot lunch too, didn't he? Shocking, I call it. If he wasn't such a nice sort of man and so clever with it, I'd be real vexed—sitting in that study, he was, for hours yesterday, ringing up Holland in that funny language of his.'

Estelle again. Eliza thanked Mrs Moore and went

back to Professor Wyllie—she might be very pretty, even a little helpless looking, but she had plenty of sound common sense; she banished Christian from her thoughts, a difficult task made easier by her patient, who, as the day proceeded, became increasingly testy. A good sign, said Doctor Trent, commenting favourably on his condition. He was to be kept at rest for a few more days, he decided, and left Eliza to the difficult job of keeping the irritable old gentleman happy. They played chess each day, a game at which she was barely passable, whereas her companion was very good indeed. But this in a way was most satisfactory, because it led to him giving her lessons, which passed the time nicely and kept him quiet, and in a few days, when he was allowed to go downstairs, Eliza cunningly offered to help him with his correspondence, which kept them both well occupied for hours on end. He had insisted, on the very first day after Christian's departure, on having the telephone plugged in by the bedside and had used it incessantly, but never as far as she knew, in order to talk to him. But he was a bad patient, and once she was out of the room there was no knowing what he did, but even though he was so trying she liked him; he had a ready sense of fun even when he wasn't feeling too well, and a mind which she envied.

They talked a good deal together, and because a restful atmosphere was so essential to him, she paid a rare visit to the village shop and purchased a traycloth and embroidery silks. She knew of no one who used such a thing, but that didn't matter. She sat with him, her pretty head bent over the fine stitches, and led him to talk of this and that, and when he became tired or bored, put her work away and got out the chessboard, or suggested in a no-nonsense voice that he needed a nap, and if she found her days dull, she gave no sign.

Soon, she supposed, she would be plunged back into the busy life of the hospital wards again and then she would be able to forget the last month for good. She grew a little quiet and thinner too, and when she telephoned her mother to explain where she was, that lady, her sharp maternal ears tuned in to every inflection of her children's voices, wanted to know what was wrong, so that Eliza had to invent a sudden cold and a lack of days off in order to lull her mother's unease.

As the Professor got better she was able to go out for longer walks, leaving the faithful Miss Trim with instructions as to what to do in an emergency, but an emergency didn't occur. Professor Wyllie continued to improve, and at the end of a week, Eliza came upon him and Doctor Trent with their heads together, deep in conversation, and the looks they cast at her were so guilty that she had no hesitation in demanding what they were cooking up between them.

'A little holiday,' explained her patient in a wheedling tone, and: 'It would do him good,' added Doctor Trent.

'Where will you go?'

'We, dear girl. Doctor Trent and—er—other advice we have sought insist that you should accompany me. Quite a short trip and just what I need to revive my interest in things. Christian van Duyl is preparing an article about our findings and would like my help. We could stay very quietly at his home.' His blue eyes studied her, as innocent as a child's. 'You could drive me in your funny little car.'

She had resolutely not thought of Christian for a whole week and it had half killed her; it was unfair that after all her efforts to forget him, he should be pushed pell-mell back into her life once more.

'It sounds just the thing for you,' she agreed, carefully noncommittal, 'but I think I must go back to St Anne's.'

'Why?'

'Well, I've been away for more than five weeks.'

'You told me yourself that you had a splendid staff nurse—they can manage quite well without you for another week or so.' He pulled down the corners of his mouth. 'I'm very upset, girl, and it's most unkind of you—now I can't go.'

'Another nurse?' she suggested, knowing that she had already lost the fight.

'No. You or no one. Go back to your precious ward and leave me here to moulder away…'

Eliza exchanged a glance with Doctor Trent, whose eyes implored her silently. 'I wouldn't do it for anyone else,' she said at length, 'but since you ask me so nicely, I see I have no choice.'

He ignored her mild sarcasm. 'Dear girl,' he beamed at her, 'what a treasure you are! I promise you that I'll be an exemplary patient, your word shall be law and I'll not wheeze once.'

She laughed then. 'I'll hold you to that, Professor, only do you feel up to arranging things with St Anne's, or do you want me to do something about it?'

'Leave it to me,' interposed Doctor Trent. 'I'll see to the details—would you like our salary paid before you go? What arrangements are usual?'

'I don't know, I don't think it's usual at all for hospital staff to be lent out, but I would like some money before I go. May I leave it to you, Doctor Trent?'

'Clothes?' asked Professor Wyllie unexpectedly.

'Well, yes—I've almost nothing with me, could I whip up to London and get a few things?'

Doctor Trent was once more helpful. 'Why not? If you could manage to get there and back tomorrow afternoon—directly after lunch, perhaps? I've a day off and will be delighted to spend the afternoon here— we're due for another game of chess, anyway.'

It was as though fate, having played her a dirty trick, was bent on compensating her for it, though she doubted whether the delight of seeing Christian again would balance the misery of parting from him and forgetting him for a second time.

She drove herself up to London the following after- noon, her thoughts in such a muddle of excitement and nervousness that it was with difficulty that she forced herself to think about clothes. Nothing much, she decided; it was still cold and wet and she didn't suppose she would go out a great deal. She packed a couple of woollen dresses and changed into a tweed suit that she had only just bought, and exchanged her topcoat for the one hanging in the wardrobe. It was a nice mixture of peat brown and green, with a green lining which matched the suit, and Eliza searched her drawers until she found a handful of woollies which would go with this outfit; she almost decided to take the mohair skirt and cashmere top, but decided against it; it was quite unlikely that she would go out in the evening and the two dresses would do for any small social occasion.

When she had finished there was still time for her to go to Men's Medical and see Mary for a few minutes before a brief, businesslike interview with Miss Smythe, who seemed quite undisturbed at the prospect of her continued absence. 'Another week or two won't matter, Sister,' she said comfortably. 'Doctor Trent telephoned me yesterday concerning your extended stay with Professor Wyllie; as far as the hospital is concerned it's perfectly in order, and I have your cheque here; he wished me to arrange that for you. Perhaps you will let me know how things go on. The Professor is far too important a person in the medical world not to command any small service which we may be able to give him.'

She smiled complacently, just as though, thought

Eliza peevishly, she was the one rendering the service. She drove back to the Professor's house a little put out, feeling in some inexplicable way that she was being pushed around by unseen forces. 'I'm nothing but a pawn,' she told herself as she parked the Fiat and went indoors, then found her ill-humour evaporating because her patient was so glad to see her back again and Mrs Moore had prepared a delicious tea for her. She had it in the sitting room while the two men finished their game, and as she munched her way through Mrs Moore's scones she speculated about Christian; for now that she was to meet him again there was no point in not thinking about him.

Supposing that when she got to his home, she found—as she suspected she might—that Estelle was quite unsuitable for him, should she do something about it? Would she be justified? Christian might not like her, but he was—had been—attracted to her; he might, just might be glad to see her again, after all. She finished the scones, polished off a slice of cherry cake and bore the tray back to the kitchen, her mind in a fine muddle, her confusion considerably increased by the delight she felt at seeing him again.

They left four days later with Professor Wyllie packed in snugly beside her, hedged about with all the safeguards necessary for the journey. They were to travel to Harwich and go aboard the night ferry; the efficient Miss Trim had dealt with everything, and now, released from her overwhelming ability and Mrs Moore's excited chatter, they were as happy as two children setting out on a treat, although Eliza, still a prey to her mixed feelings, wasn't sure if the trip would turn out to be a treat or a trial. Time would tell, she told herself, taking refuge in clichés, and did her best to enter into her companions's high spirits.

They had a surprisingly smooth crossing and the Professor at least slept the night through, and if he noticed that Eliza was rather hollow-eyed when they met for an early breakfast, he said nothing, only chatted interestingly about Holland. 'You'll like the country around Nijmegen,' he told her, 'wooded here and there and far more character to it than the rest of the country. Christian lives outside the city—it's on the German border, you know, but his home is on the Dutch side and very rural.'

She tried to speak casually. 'What is the village called?'

'Well, there isn't a village, just a hamlet. The nearest village is Horssen and that's no size at all. But with a car, of course, it's an easy matter to get to Nijmegen in ten minutes or so.'

'Isn't that inconvenient for his practice?'

Her companion blinked rapidly behind his spectacles. 'Shouldn't think so; he's got a car, you know.' For some reason he laughed and didn't tell her why.

It was an easy drive from the Hoek once she had negotiated the nightmare of Rotterdam and come out

safely on to the E96 on the other side. She found the
motorway dull enough, and her companion agreed with
her, pointing out that the real Holland lay in the small
towns and villages they bypassed on their hundred-mile
journey, but when they stopped for coffee, two miles on
the further side of Gorinchem, they found a small café
close to the River Waal, and sat watching the long barges
making their slow way up and down its busy waters. The
little houses around them were peaceful under the winter
sky and across the water there were windmills turning.

They went on again presently, back to the motorway,
until they crossed the river at Tiel and took a more
peaceful road. 'For there is no need to go all the way into
Nijmegen,' explained Professor Wyllie. 'We can get to
Christian's home from this end—keep on this road as far
as Druten and I'll tell you where to go when we're there—
it's through the place, the first turning on your right.'

The country was pretty now, even in winter, with the
river coming into view every now and then and wooded
land between the fields. Eliza drove through Druten and
obedient to her companion's direction, turned off the
road into a country lane bordered by grassland at first,
then gradually becoming screened with shrubs and trees.

'Next turning on your left,' counselled the Professor.
'Look for two pillars with creatures on top of them.'

A strange sort of road, thought Eliza, as she nosed
the little car between the two tall red brick columns, and
caught a glimpse of dragon-like creatures crowning

their tops as they went past. 'How far?' she wanted to know. 'It's a narrow road…'

Her companion grunted as she took a bend a little too fast, bringing into a view a large and splendid house.

'Oh, a research centre,' she declared. 'I suppose Professor van Duyl has his headquarters here.'

'You might say that, I suppose. Stop at the front door, girl.'

There was a sweep of steps to climb—slowly, because of the Professor's wheezing, so that by the time they had reached the imposing door it had been opened—by Hub.

He greeted them in his usual manner, but he looked different; at Inverpolly he had been used to wearing what most of the men wore, a thick sweater and corduroy or tweed slacks, but now he was nattily attired in a black jacket, pinstripe trousers, very white linen and a bow tie. He took the Professor's outstretched hand and shook it and when Eliza proffered hers, shook that too, bowing just a little as he did so. Probably a Dutch custom, thought Eliza. 'I had no idea that you worked here too,' she observed with interest, but beyond smiling and nodding he said nothing but ushered them into the lobby and from thence into the hall.

It was vast and lofty, with a magnificent staircase leading to a half landing and then winging away on either side to a remote upstairs. There were tapestries on the walls and the furniture, Eliza observed, was very grand. A showplace, owned by some hard-up member of the Dutch aristocracy and rented to the medical profession, although it looked like a stately home. At any moment, she felt sure, a door would open and a guide would appear and start to intone the beauties of her surroundings. And indeed a door did open, but not to admit a guide; it was Christian who crossed the expanse of marble floor with the assured air of the polite host. Anyone would think that he owned the place, she thought, watching him. He looked handsomer than ever and was, as usual, faultlessly turned out. She was suddenly glad that she was wearing the new tweed outfit and the Rayne's shoes she hadn't been able to afford…

He had reached them by now, shaking Professor Wyllie by the hand, welcoming him. 'You are wonderfully recovered,' he observed, and turned to look at Eliza, 'due no doubt to our redoubtable Miss Proudfoot.'

She stared at his face; his dark eyes were alight with laughter. And what had he to laugh about? she wondered uneasily. She could feel her heart thumping away under the new tweeds like a demented thing; whether meeting her again amused him or not, she was overjoyed to see him; she knew now that however hard she tried she would never be able to forget him. She said quietly: 'How do you do, Professor,' and offered a hand, mindful of the Dutch custom of shaking hands on all and every occasion, and Christian was Dutch as well as being back in his own country.

He took the hand and didn't let it go. 'Welcome to my home, Eliza,' he said, and now she knew why he had looked so amused.

Her eyes rounded with astonishment. She declared: 'Your home? all this?' she waved her free hand at the magnificence around them and choked a little. 'And I gave you a broom to clean out the cottage, and you mopped the floor!'

'Rather well, I thought.'

She wriggled her hand a little and his grip tightened. 'And Hub? Does he live here too?'

'Of course—he orders my house for me; he's my right-hand man—a paragon amongst men and a lifelong friend as well.' He laughed a little. 'I think that in England you would call him the butler, but to us he is much more than that.'

'Oh, yes, I know.' Eliza looked at Professor Wyllie, standing beside her, oozing benevolence, his blue eyes missing nothing. 'You didn't tell me,' she accused him gently.

'No need, girl—why should I? What's it to you, anyway?'

A forthright statement which left her without words, so that Christian came to her rescue with a suggestion that she might like to go to her room, nodding at Hub as he spoke. 'We lunch at half past twelve and my mother is most anxious to meet you.'

Hub, who had disappeared, returned, trailing in his

wake a tall angular girl who answered to the name of Nel, and led Eliza up the great staircase, to take the left-hand wing which opened on to a wide corridor where she opened a door and waved Eliza smilingly inside. Left alone, Eliza saw that her case was already there, quite dwarfed by its surroundings, for the room reflected the magnificence of the hall. If Christian had hoped to impress her he had succeeded very well. She wandered round, picking up delicate silver, bric-à-brac and china, smelling at the bowl of flowers, fingering the books which someone had thoughtfully placed at the bedside, examining the window hangings and the bedspread on the bed with its important carved head-board. It was all quite beautiful and not quite to be believed. She turned away from its satinwood and pastel brocades and went to the window, which afforded a view of a large formal garden, which even at this dreary time of year looked pleasant, with its sunken pond and statues and straight paths and clipped hedges, but the sight of it did nothing to quieten her thoughts. She went back to the dressing table and tidied herself for lunch, and presently, outwardly serene, but inwardly scared to death, she went downstairs.

Hub was in the hall; she suspected that he had been waiting for her, for he came to her at once. 'In here, miss,' he advised her, with a kind of benevolent encouragement, just as though he knew that she was nervous, and threw open a handsome pair of doors.

She had expected another vast room, hung with brocade and family portraits and furnished with chairs, which, while extremely handsome to look at, would be most uncomfortable in which to sit, but it was nothing like that at all—a smallish room, glowing with colour and chintz-covered chairs, with a bright fire in the steel grate and under her feet a rich carpet, inches thick, all combining to give an air of great cosiness. There seemed to be a great many people, but only at first glance, for as Christian came towards her from the group around the fire, she saw that there were only five other people in the room besides the two of them. Professor Wyllie, of course, and not surprisingly, Doctor Berrevoets and Doctor Peters. And an elderly lady, not much taller than herself and still pretty.

The fifth person was a young woman, tall and rather angular, whom Eliza had no difficulty in recognising. Here then was Estelle, exactly like her photograph, excepting that it hadn't revealed her extreme slimness. No shape at all, Eliza summed up, but good-looking in a mediaeval kind of way, expensively dressed too, though what was the use of gorgeous clothes if there were no curves for them to cling to? Eliza, who had some quite satisfactory curves of her own, felt more cheerful as she murmured at Christian and was introduced to his mother. She liked the little lady immediately; she had her son's dark eyes, but there the resemblance ended; he must take after his father, she glanced at the portrait hanging above her hostess's head and knew that she was right; there was the stare, the good looks, the powerful nose with its winged nostrils. She answered Mevrouw van Duyl's gentle questions, put in excellent English, and at the touch of Christian's hand went to meet Estelle.

She had been right; now that she was close to her and actually talking, Estelle seemed more mediaeval than at first. She had a long straight nose and pale blue eyes, large and thickly lashed, but they held no expression except well-bred interest—perhaps they would light up when she was alone with Christian. Eliza's own eyes sparkled at the very idea so that Doctor Peters, standing by Estelle, was constrained to remark upon her evident good health. After that she went to talk to Doctor Berrevoets, and found herself beside him at lunch, taken in a room which could have housed half a dozen tables of the size at which they sat. She ate her way through the delicious meal, answering composedly when spoken to, but not contributing to the conversation, for somehow Estelle, without saying a word, had managed to convey to her the fact that she was the nurse and only there because they were all too well-mannered to dwell on the fact that she was paid wages and was hardly out of the same drawer, socially speaking. So silly, Eliza chided herself silently, to mind what Estelle thought about her. She wished that she was a little nearer Mevrouw van Duyl, who, although she treated her with the utmost kindness, was separated from her by a vast expanse of white table-cloth—and one couldn't shout.

She got up from the table with relief and overriding her patient's ill-tempered remarks about being bullied, led him away to his room for a much-needed nap. She didn't go downstairs again; her room was warm and comfortable and there were books to read. Someone had been in and unpacked while she had been at lunch and after a few minutes' idle reading she found her writing case and sat down to compose a letter; her parents would be interested to hear about the house and its treasures. She had almost finished it when there was a knock on the door and Estelle came in.

'Christian thought that you might like to walk in the garden,' she said in her precise English. 'If we put on coats and scarves it will be pleasant enough.'

Eliza got her coat and found a scarf; she didn't want to go walking with Estelle, but on the other hand it might give her the chance to find out more about her— there must be something which attracted Christian, and she had to admit that she had been prejudiced against her, and now would be the time to find out what Estelle was really like.

They went out of the side door which led them straight to the formal garden, and Eliza began to ask, rather feverishly, a great many questions about it; she suspected that she and Estelle would have very little in common and gardens were usually a safe topic.

Estelle talked intelligently but without much interest. They stayed out of doors for half an hour, and at the end of that time Eliza had confirmed her suspicion that the girl was a bore—nice enough, she supposed, friendly even, but she showed no emotion about anything; Eliza had unconsciously put that to the test, for, seeing a mole emerging from his hill, she had squealed with delight and would have stayed motionless for minutes in the hope that he might reappear, only a glance at her companion's face showed only too plainly that to Estelle, moles were of no interest at all, moreover there was no need to become vulgarly excited about them.

Feeling quite subdued, Eliza followed her back into the house, this time through a conservatory full of spring flowers over which she would have liked to linger. But she was given no opportunity to do this, being taken into a handsome room with a good deal of gilding on its walls and a great many chairs and little tables, where Mevrouw van Duyl was sitting by the fire. She looked up and smiled as they went in and said kindly: 'There you are, my dears—you are not too cold, I hope? Tomorrow, Eliza—I may call you that?—I will take you round the house if you are interested. It is a great awkward place, but quite beautiful—at least we think so, although it is far too big for the two of us.'

Estelle had seated herself on the other side of the chimneypiece. 'You forget, Mevrouw van Duyl, that when Christian and I are married, I shall be living here too.' She spoke gently, but Eliza saw the older lady wince and frown, though the face she turned to her was quite placid. 'Sit down, Eliza,' she was bidden, 'and tell me about yourself, for Christian has hardly mentioned you and I had not the least idea that you were so young and pretty.'

Eliza, aware that Estelle was listening to this challenging remark even though she had picked up a magazine, excused herself. 'I should like that, Mevrouw van Duyl, but perhaps another time? It's time I got Professor Wyllie on his feet again; if I let him sleep too long, he gets cross.'

Her hostess smiled. 'Of course, Eliza. I forget that you are a nurse—you do not look like one, you see, and somehow, from the little Christian said of you, I imagined you to be middle-aged and plain.'

All three of them laughed and Eliza hoped that her merriment sounded real, for it was nothing of the sort. Going upstairs to the Professor's room presently it struck her that however unsuitable Estelle was, she couldn't carry out her intention of bringing the match to an end and marrying Christian herself; she hadn't known then that he was the owner of this vast house and living in the lap of luxury; he might be a hard-working doctor and a successful one too, but he didn't belong to her world, but Estelle did and that was why he had chosen her to be his wife. She would make him a very good wife, but whether she would make him happy was a moot point. She was very quiet as she got her patient out of bed and tidied up the room. He was still a little irritable and his pulse was too high, but she knew better than to dissuade him from doing what he wished with the rest of the day. A long chat with the other men, he told her with glee; it would be most interesting, and she should hear all about it later. 'And I'll have my tea up here,' he decided. 'Ring that bell and ask for it, Eliza, and have a cup with me.'

She was only too glad to do so, for she had been dreading going back to the drawing room; a chat with Mevrouw van Duyl would have been nice, but an hour of Estelle's company, trying to find something to talk about, wasn't tempting.

They had their tea and presently, when he had gone downstairs, she went back to her room, finished her letter and then, uncertain of the evening ahead, bathed and changed into one of the woollen dresses, dove grey with a high white collar and little cuffs. It was a very plain dress, save for the silk bow under her chin, but it was suitable for after six in a quiet sort of way, and anyway, she wasn't quite sure of her status; was she a guest, or was she to be considered as Professor Wyllie's nurse? There was a difference, quite a large one; when she saw him again she would have to ask him.

She spent time on her face and hair because she had nothing else to do—indeed, she took her hair down again and started brushing it out with the idea of trying another style. The knock on the door was unexpected, but Hub's anxious face and urgent voice brought her to her feet at once.

'It's Professor Wyllie, miss—if you would go to the library right away.'

She had taken the precaution of bringing the portable oxygen with her as well as the drugs he might need and syringes and needles; she had laid them out ready on a linenfold dower chest standing at the foot of the bed; now she snatched them up and was flying downstairs almost before Hub had finished speaking.

She knew where the library was; Estelle had pointed it out to her as they had left the house that afternoon. She opened the door and walked in. Professor Wyllie was sitting in a large armchair, having what she could see was a nasty attack. Christian was bending over him, loosening his tie, while the other two doctors stood nearby, looking helpless. She skipped past them, offered her neat little parcel of phials and syringes to Christian, got the oxygen started and applied it to Professor Wyllie's anxious face. 'Better in a moment,' she assured him soothingly. 'We're going to get you out of that jacket.' She turned round to engage help from Doctor Peters and thus missed the look on Christian's face; when she did have time to look at him, he was gravely checking the injection before plunging it into his colleague's arm. The result was dramatic; within a few minutes the old man was breathing easily once more and giving testy instructions as to what would be done next, to none of which Christian paid the least attention.

'Bed for you, sir,' he ordered in a quiet voice which brooked no refusal. 'Eliza, go ahead and see that it's ready, would you?' He went to the door with her and as he opened it, murmured: 'You weren't going to bed, by any chance?'

She had forgotten that her hair was hanging loose and that her feet were still in the pink quilted mules someone or other had given her for Christmas. Under his amused gaze she went a delicate pink. 'Of course not!' she snapped, and whisked past him.

She had the bed ready by the time they had borne the protesting Professor upstairs, and with Christian's help, got him into it. 'Would you stay five minutes?' she asked, and flew to her own room to get into the uniform she had brought with her; at least her evening was settled for her now.

And Christian, when he saw her in her cap and apron once more, said nothing—probably he had expected it, or welcomed it as a solution of a delicate problem, for she felt sure that whatever he felt about it, Estelle, in the nicest possible way, would have pointed out to him that she was a nurse, not a guest.

But she had reckoned without her host. The dinner gong had hardly ceased to sound when there was a knock on the door and Hub came in.

'You are to go down to dinner, miss,' he told her,

looking paternally at her. 'I will stay with the Professor and let you know if anything should occur.'

She glanced at the sleeping figure on the bed. 'Oh, Hub, that's very good of you, but I'd much rather stay up here—if I could have something on a tray?' She smiled at him. 'That's if no one would mind.'

'But I do mind very much.' Christian had followed Hub into the room. 'You will give us the pleasure of your company downstairs, Eliza.' He came across the room to her and took her arm. 'You know as well as I do that Professor Wyllie will be perfectly all right again; a day in bed and he will be as he usually is, and Hub knows exactly what he must do in an emergency.'

'Yes—but I'm the Professor's nurse, that's why I came. Besides, I'm in uniform.'

He smiled at her and her heart rocked. 'And very nice too, though I found your previous outfit most eye-catching.' He had walked her across the room and out of the door, which Hub closed silently behind them.

'Oh, please, I really would rather not...'

He took no notice at all, only said strangely: 'I wish we were back at Inverpolly,' and bent to kiss her swiftly, then, still holding her arm, went down the stairs beside her, silent now, just as she was, for surprise had taken her tongue.

CHAPTER EIGHT

ELIZA was glad, when she saw Estelle, that she had got back into uniform again, for the little grey wool dress would have been entirely eclipsed by that young lady's long crêpe gown, an expensive garment, thought Eliza, running an experienced female eye over it, beautifully cut but far too low in the neck for those regrettable salt-cellars. If Estelle didn't put on a few pounds soon, she would be skinny by the time she was forty. Eliza, in her mind's eye, knew just how she would look, but perhaps Christian liked thin women. Her thoughts shied away from him; it was no time to reflect upon his kiss. Instead, she made small talk with Doctor Berrevoets and drank her sherry before going to talk to Mevrouw van Duyl, who carried on with the small talk in her kindly way while her dark eyes took stock of Eliza, and presently they held the same amused gleam which showed from time to time in her son's eyes. Eliza didn't see that, but presently when they were on the point of going to the dining room, he left Estelle's side and lingered a moment with his parent.

'What gives you that delightfully satisfied expression, Mama? You look like the cat who discovered the cream.'

She patted his arm and gave him a wide smile. 'Dear boy,' she said, and then: 'Talking of cats—I'm sure Eliza would love to go and see that quaint little animal you brought back with you. Such a dear girl, and you never told me how very pretty she was. Perhaps you could take her to see the little animals after dinner, and I daresay you would like a little talk, too.'

It was her son's turn to smile. 'Dear Mama,' he spoke very mildly, 'how you must have delighted Father with your little plots!'

'Yes, dear—and you are so like him.' She looked suddenly downcast. 'It was only one of my silly notions, a—a daydream.'

He looked at her with fondness. 'Yes, dearest, but do not allow yourself to forget that Estelle and I plan to marry within the next few months.'

'No, Christian, I never forget that. Such a pleasant girl, and so capable, sometimes it seems to me that she had already taken over the running of this house when she comes to stay—of course she does it beautifully.'

His mouth hardened. 'Quite so, Mama. Now, since everyone is waiting…'

Eliza sat next to Doctor Berrevoets with Christian, at the head of the table, on her other side, but it was quickly apparent to her that conversation between them was to be limited to platitudes, uttered at sufficiently frequent intervals to escape sheer neglect. It was Estelle, on his other side, who received the lion's share of his attention, although what she said to interest him, in Eliza's opinion, could have been put on a postage stamp and room to spare, nor was his attention in the least lover-like—she noted that while inclining her neatly capped head towards Doctor Berrevoets, listening to his dissertation on butterflies. The study of them was his hobby and he was delighted to find such a ready listener. She knew nothing of the pretty creatures, although she could recognise a Red Admiral or a Cabbage White, but she gave him almost all of her attention, the remaining bit of it being focused on Christian and Estelle: she could see no sign of any deep feeling between them. True, Christian was hardly a man to demonstrate his affections in public, but no one, least of all herself who was so in love with him, could have failed to mistake the look of a man in love. And there was no such look, she was quite sure of that, and as for Estelle, if she had any feelings at all, she was keeping them well concealed.

It was a pity that he wasn't an ordinary GP with not much money and an ordinary house; then she would have done her best to rescue him from a marriage which she was certain would be disastrous, but that was impossible now. Estelle, for all her tepid nature, had all the attributes required of her; she would be an excellent hostess, know all the right people, never lose her temper and know exactly what to do even in the most awkward situation. She would never let him down, she would certainly not expect him to rescue her off mountains because she would never be fool enough to go there in the first place, neither would she given him a broom and tell him to sweep... Eliza caught Doctor Berrevoets' eye, fixed expectantly on her, and she hadn't the slightest idea what he had been saying.

'You're quite right,' said Christian, speaking across her, coming to her rescue with all the ease of an accomplished host. 'Very few people realise that the female Blue Butterfly is in fact brown. Personally, I find the Holly Blue particularly lovely.'

'Ah, yes,' said Doctor Berrevoets happily, '*Celastrina Argiolus*, quite charming. I was just telling Eliza that when she goes home she must use her eyes.'

'Indeed, yes.' Christian's voice was bland, as was his face. 'I have observed, though, that she does that to good effect.' He smiled at her and she glared at him, a futile gesture quite lost on him. 'And that reminds me, my mother is sure that you will want to see Cat and the kittens, they have settled in very nicely; my own cats have quite taken to her and so has the kitchen cat. She has a basket in my study—perhaps you would like to see her presently?'

'Oh, please. I did wonder...but there hasn't been much opportunity to ask. But I knew they'd be comfortable here.'

They went back to the drawing room for their coffee after that, and this time Eliza found herself sitting beside Mevrouw van Duyl, but not for long; Christian joined them within a few minutes. 'Estelle and I are going to take Eliza to see Cat,' he told his mother, and Eliza watched the two pairs of eyes, so dark and alike, meet and wondered why he should give his mother a faintly mocking smile.

Cat remembered her and offered a small head for a caress. She looked sleek and content, quite another animal from the poor bedraggled thing Christian had hauled into the cottage, and Eliza told her so, picking her up to cuddle her, while the kittens, their eyes open now, stared unblinkingly up at her.

'Oh, aren't they sweet?' She was down on her knees now, tickling their chins. 'You'd never think, looking at her now, that she'd been half starved—and so wet!' She chuckled. 'Do you remember how frightened I was when she tapped on the window?' She laughed up at Christian and found him looking at her, his face alight and warm.

'You certainly sounded terrified.' He was sitting on his heels beside her now and Cat was wreathing herself round him. 'She's turned into a charming little creature.'

'There are already three cats in the house as well as a dog,' Estelle, standing behind them, pointed out in a reasonable voice. 'Surely we might find good homes for them?'

'They have a good home here.' Christian's voice was quiet, but Eliza sensed his impatience at the remark.

She put the kittens down and got to her feet. 'I don't suppose they'll bother anyone,' she offered placatingly, 'I mean, they quickly learn where they're allowed to go and who…' She stopped awkwardly and Estelle took her up, still in an agreeable voice.

'You make me sound a hard-hearted person.'

'Oh, I'm sorry, I didn't mean that at all. I know you'll be very kind to them.'

'Certainly I shall, as long as they stay in their right place. I have never been able to understand sentimentality in the treatment of animals.' Estelle sat down in a high-backed chair, looking complacent, and went on: 'It will be my duty as mistress of this house to see that all its occupants are properly cared for, a duty for which I feel myself eminently suited.' She closed her eyes as she spoke—and a good thing too, for Eliza was regarding her open-mouthed and Christian's face had the look of a man who is teetering on the edge of a very high cliff. By the time she had opened her eyes again they had normal expressions on their faces and she continued: 'I discovered a book the other day, a child's book by someone called Beatrix Potter.' She wrinkled her patrician nose in faint disgust. 'Animals, dressed like people! I must say that I found it most extraordinary.'

'In Dutch? How marvellous—I had no idea they were translated into Dutch.' Eliza was quite carried away with the idea. 'The Flopsy Bunnies and Jemima Puddleduck…'

'Mrs Tiggywinkle and Tom Kitten,' said Christian.

'You know them too? I was brought up on them, I think they were the first books I learned to read.'

'My favourite bedtime reading,' remembered the Professor, 'my mother has them still.' They smiled at each other, sharing pleasant memories, and Estelle said sharply: 'Should we not go back to our guests, Christian? I am sure Eliza wishes to go back to her patient.'

There was the faintest hint of annoyance in her voice, and Eliza said at once, 'Yes, I do. Thank you for letting me visit Cat, it's nice to see her happy.' She got herself to the door. 'Good night. Would you please say good night to the rest of them for me?'

She was through the door and half way up the staircase before they followed her out of the study; she was too far away to hear what they were saying, but Christian sounded annoyed.

The Professor was dozing lightly and Hub came quietly to meet her.

'There was no need for you to come back yet, miss; Professor van Duyl said that I was to stay until you came up to bed.'

'How kind, Hub, but there are one or two things I want to do. I've been to see Cat and the kittens.'

'Settled down very well, if I might say so, miss. Professor van Duyl took care of that, very anxious he was to have the little beasts comfortable. Sits in his study, he does, working, and they sit there with him— them and Willy the dog. Very fond of him he is too.'

'The Alsatian—I've not seen him, Hub.'

'Well, miss, Juffrouw van der Daal doesn't like him overmuch, so he's in the kitchen now. The Professor takes him out as usual of course, and he was in the library with the gentlemen this afternoon, but you wouldn't have noticed him under the desk. When we're on our own he has the run of the house.'

Eliza heard the wistfulness in his voice. 'I hope I see him before I go back, Hub.'

'I'm sure you will, miss. Would the Professor like a light supper presently?'

'Oh, yes, please. Shall I come down for it?'

He looked shocked. 'Oh, no, miss. Someone will bring it up, and perhaps you would ring when you want the tray removed. Soup? A morsel of fish? And I believe Cook has some excellent water ices.'

'Oh, yes—I had some at dinner, they were delicious. That would do very well, Hub, I'm not sure what the Professor should drink, though. Tonic water's a bit dull, isn't it?'

'A little fresh fruit juice, perhaps?' And when she nodded, he smiled paternally and went quietly away. He was a dear, she thought, as she went to sit by the bed and picked up her embroidery and began to stitch so that when her patient woke up he wouldn't think that she was just sitting there waiting impatiently for him to open his eyes.

He wakened very shortly afterwards, irritable and inclined to snap her head off, but the arrival of supper caused him to brighten considerably. Only her offer of the fruit juice sent him into a fit of the sulks, which she was doing her best to weather when the door opened and Christian came in. He had a bottle in one hand and glasses in the other.

'Ah, just in time, I see. I met Hub in the hall and he told me that he had just served fruit juice with your supper, something which I felt should be remedied at once.'

He put the glasses down on a small table, a delicate trifle of rosewood inlaid with mother-of-pearl, and set to work on the bottle's cork.

Professor Wyllie, all at once sunny-tempered as a happy baby, watched him, and Eliza watched him too. He dominated the room, just as he did any company and any room without making any conscious effort to do so. For some reason that simple fact made her feel that all was right with her world, although common sense told her that this was not so. The next few days weren't going to be particularly happy ones, Estelle didn't like her and although good manners would prevent her from saying so out loud, she would make sure that Eliza would never forget that she was the nurse and not a guest.

'I shall come up here tomorrow, sir,' observed Christian easily. 'We can just as easily work on that article with you here in bed as downstairs.' He glanced at Eliza. 'A pity you don't type, dear girl.'

'I do.'

'Splendid. You can keep an eye on our patient and

type the thing for us.' He handed them each a glass. 'Your health, sir.'

The elder man beamed. 'A splendid idea, though a little boring for Eliza.'

The dark eyes were fixed on her face and she made haste to stare down into her glass. 'Then we must recompense her, must we not? A drive round the countryside, perhaps, or a trip to Nijmegen. Which would you prefer, Eliza?'

'I really don't mind. Besides, it would take up your time—there must be other things…'

'There are. What do you think of the champagne?'

'It's very nice,' she told him sedately, and heard the old man laugh.

'Heidsieck Monopole—Diamant Bleu 1961. Am I right, Christian?'

'You are.' He had gone to sit down, disposing his length in a comfortable fashion which suggested that he had come to stay. Eliza put down her glass and picked up her needlework once more. She feared that the champagne would go to her head; they had, after all, had wine with their dinner; she thought it was a burgundy, but she wasn't sure. As though he had read her thoughts, Christian continued, 'We had a Corton Charlemagne 1966 at dinner—a splendid white burgundy, don't you agree?—you shall sample it when you come down.'

'There was no need for champagne, dear boy.' The

Professor was chumping away at his fish, in a splendid good humour.

'You're wrong. I'm celebrating something.'

'May we know?' Professor Wyllie asked the question and Eliza echoed it silently. They had decided the date of the wedding, they would be married immediately…her thoughts ran riot. Why had she ever come, she must have been mad… Her fragmental ideas were swept tidily away by his answer.

'No. No one knows.' He got to his feet slowly. 'I'll wish you both good night.'

The room seemed empty when he had gone, and very quiet. Eliza went on stitching, making conversation with her patient, and when he had finished his supper, suggested that he might like a game of cards. 'Or better still, there's a table here for chess or draughts.'

They played a mild game or so of draughts and Eliza, busy with her thoughts, allowed him to win before getting him ready for bed; arranging his pillows how he liked them, setting the bell close at hand, and turning out all but a small table lamp. 'I'm not in the least tired,' she lied cheerfully to him, 'and there's a book I want to dip into—do you mind if I bring it in here for half an hour?'

He smiled at her very nicely. 'What a dear child you are! Afraid that I'm going to start another wheeze? I promise you I won't, but I shall enjoy your company. Get the book by all means.'

He was already sleepy and when she returned from her room he had his eyes closed, to open them once to bid her good night. 'You're a great comfort to me, Eliza,' he told her.

She had taken off her cap and put on her pink sippers again. The house was very quiet, but then in a house of that size, she reminded herself, it would be hard to hear voices from downstairs. She moved her chair cautiously a little nearer the lamp and opened John Donne.

She didn't hear Christian come in; something made her look up to see him standing there, just inside the door, watching her. He crossed the room with surprising lightness considering his size and bent down to whisper: 'Why are you not in bed?'

'Well,' her voice was a mere thread of sound, 'I wanted to be quite sure.'

He didn't answer her but took the book from her hand and studied. She had been reading *The Broken Heart* and he stared down at the page before handing it back to her and then, his mouth very close to her ear: 'Beatrix Potter—and now John Donne.'

'I have a very catholic taste,' she assured him seriously.

'But not, I hope, a broken heart?'

She returned his piercing look steadily, her mouth firmly closed against the things she wished to say to him and could not; she shook her head instead and crossed her fingers unseen because although she hadn't said a word, it was the same as telling a lie.

'Strange,' his whisper was fierce in her ear. 'I imagined that you had.'

Eliza didn't look up; her eyes were fixed on John Donne lying in her lap. They focused on the end of the poem: 'My ragges of heart can like, wish and adore, but after one such love, can love no more.' Donne had hit the nail on the head; her heart wasn't just broken, it was in rags too.

'And what do you think of Estelle?' The whisper had become silky.

She spoke to the book. 'She is charming—and very handsome.'

'She will be a splendid hostess, don't you think? and run my home, sit on local committees and be the Lady Bountiful, as would be expected of my wife—the kind of wife I thought I wanted, Eliza. My mother will have time on her hands, will she not? I hadn't realized quite how much. Estelle has money too—she won't need my millions.'

Eliza's startled eyes flew to his face. 'Not millions—money millions?'

He grinned. 'Indeed I'm afraid so—in guldens, of course, in England I am merely a wealthy man.'

He wasn't joking. Eliza swallowed and said woodenly, 'Well, you have a large house to maintain.'

He shrugged. 'Perhaps you don't approve?'

'Why ever not? It's a beautiful house and the things in it are beautiful too. It would be terrible if you couldn't look after it all.'

He fetched a chair and set it down opposite her and bestrode it, his arms folded across its back. 'Did you notice Estelle's ring?'

How silly men were; didn't they know that a girl always noticed things like that within the first few seconds? 'It's magnificent.'

He shook his head. 'Diamonds in a modern setting, but Estelle wanted it. The family betrothal ring is old-fashioned; rose diamonds and rubies set in gold—all the wives have worn it and there are earrings to match, given to each successive bride as a wedding gift. Estelle wants earrings to match her ring.'

'I expect they will look very nice,' Eliza whispered in a tepid voice, and then, carried away by curiosity, went on: 'What are you celebrating?'

Christian fixed her with a dark look. 'Ah, so you're interested, are you? That at least is something. I shan't tell you.' He grinned again and suddenly unable to bear the conversation any longer she got up. 'I think if you don't mind, I might go to bed now.'

He stood up too. 'Do that, Eliza, but before you go to sleep, lie in your bed and remember everything I have said. Don't bother to recall your part of the conversation; most of it wasn't true, anyway.'

He opened the door for her after she had taken a quick peep at the sleeping form in the bed and wished her a whispered good night, but for some stupid reason she wanted to cry. She nodded her head at him instead, her eyes very wide to hold back the tears.

She was up early, in fact she was dressed when Nel came in with her morning tea. Eliza took her cup to the window and stood looking out on to the garden, bleak in the half darkness of the grey morning, and when she had finished it she went quietly along to Professor Wyllie's room. He was awake, bright-eyed and refreshed after a good night's sleep, and was all for getting up straight away. Fortunately Hub arrived with his morning tea and with it a message for Eliza. 'Would you care to join Professor van Duyl downstairs, miss? He thought you might enjoy a quick walk with him and Willy.'

One of the conclusions Eliza had come to during the night had been that of not seeing more of Christian than she must; instantly forgotten as she settled Professor Wyllie against the pillows, begged him to be good and ran to her room to fetch her cloak.

Christian was in the hall with Willy sitting patiently beside him. She was wished a good morning, introduced to the great beast and ushered down a narrow passage to a side door. 'I saw your light,' explained the Professor as they went through it into the chilly day and turned away from the house, down a flagstoned path between shrubs and trees. At the end of it there was a wall with a little wooden door and when they emerged on the other side Eliza saw that they were in a small park. 'Is this yours too?' she wanted to know.

'Yes.' He was walking along at a great rate, so that she was forced to skip a step or two to keep up. Willy was already out of sight and after a minute or two she asked: 'Do you have a surgery here?'

'No, though everyone hereabouts knows that I'm always available if I'm home. I have a room in one of the cottages in the village and go there three times a week, but my consulting rooms are in Nijmegen. I go there every day, but not today.'

'You work in the hospital there as well?'

'Oh, yes.' He had slowed his stride and taken her arm. 'I've beds at the hospitals in Appeldorn and Arnhem, and a couple in Utrecht.'

'But you can have very little leisure.' Somehow she had never suspected that he was so wrapped up in his work.

'I like it that way.' Something in his voice stopped her asking any more questions, so she said instead: 'Willy's a wonderful dog,' and whistled to him so that he came tearing across the grass towards her. She bent to scratch his ears. 'Does he go everywhere with you?'

'Yes. He sits under my desk during surgery hours and guards the car while I'm on my visits.'

'He must miss you very much when you're away from home.'

'He does, though my mother dotes on him.' They had come to another wall, with a little wicket gate in it which he opened. 'We can go through here and walk round to the other end and come in through the front drive,' he told her. 'And now tell me, what are your plans?'

'Plans? I haven't any. I'll go back to St Anne's, to my job on Men's Medical, as soon as Professor Wyllie is well enough—that will be within a few days, I suppose.'

'Eager to get back?' His voice was blandly enquiring and she made haste to say: 'Of course not,' and then, in case he began to ask awkward questions: 'Is it colder here than in England during the winter?'

His mouth twitched very slightly. 'Yes, on the whole I think it is,' and he launched into a lengthy discourse about atmospheric pressures, isobars and meteorologist's forecasts which set her head reeling. It lasted until they were walking up the drive, and only ceased as they reached the bend in the drive where the house came so magnificently into view. 'Like it?' he asked her.

'It's super. When I saw it for the first time, it took my breath. It must be wonderful to live here—to make it your home.'

'It is.' He whistled to Willy, who joined them at once, walking soberly at his master's heels. 'We'll go in through the kitchen entrance so that Willy can be dried off.'

She went with him round to the back of the house and across a cobbled courtyard to a low wooden door, and then along a brick-floored passage and so to the kitchen, a large room with a great many doors and occupied by a number of people bustling about. Cat and the kittens were in their basket before the Aga stove and Willy, barely giving Hub time to rub him down, went to settle himself beside her. Eliza said good morning to the watching faces and saw them all smiling, and when Christian said something to them in Dutch they answered him cheerfully. They looked happy and contented and were obviously on good terms with him. It would be nice, she mused, to own a house such as this one and have these cheerful people to work for you in it.

They were back in the hall, climbing the staircase, when she observed:

'You have a lot of people working here.'

He said casually: 'Oh, yes—they live here too; it is their home.'

And she remembered how, when she had first known him, she had thought him to be arrogant and ill-tempered and uncaring of other people. He wasn't; he minded about these people who so obviously liked and respected him; probably they loved the place as much as he did.

They parted on the landing, richly carpeted and hung with portraits on its silk-panelled walls. 'Breakfast in half an hour,' he told her with a friendly smile, and opened Professor Wyllie's door for her.

It surprised her to find everyone in the breakfast room when she at last found it; no one had mentioned that there was such a place and she had gone to the dining room and found it deserted, its table, its mahogany gleaming, devoid of cloth and cutlery. She went back into the hall, supposing that she would have to listen at all the doors until she heard voices, when Hub came from the kitchen and with an apology, opened a door for her. It made matters worse to find that those seated at table were already half way through their meal, and Estelle's gentle good morning, coupled with her swift glance at the clock, was hard to bear.

Eliza sat down and addressed herself to her hostess. 'I'm sorry I'm late,' she explained. 'I didn't know that breakfast was in this room, I went to the dining room.'

The dark eyes twinkled kindly. 'It is I who should be sorry, Eliza, for not telling you. In any case breakfast is eaten when we wish to eat it, there is no strict time for it.'

A remark which put her at her ease, although she could see that Estelle didn't agree with that at all. Probably when she was mistress of the house, everyone would have to be in their places on the dot. She peeped at Christian, sitting immersed in his post and the newspapers; with all her heart she longed for him to become suddenly poor so that Estelle wouldn't marry him after all. No, that wouldn't do, for the girl had money of her own, he had said so. It would have to be the house, taken from him by some dramatic stroke of misfortune—because that was why Estelle had said she would marry him, Eliza guessed; no girl in her senses would miss such an opportunity of becoming its mistress—a thunderbolt, perhaps, or a long-lost heir who returned from the dead to claim his rightful heritage... Her colourful imagination ran riot and was only checked when Christian addressed her. 'Will ten o'clock suit you, Eliza?'

She said: 'Yes, Professor,' in a meek voice and went on with her dreaming. No, he couldn't give up the house; he loved it, and it was quite unchristian of her to wish that Estelle could drop dead. She sighed, so loudly that several pairs of eyes were turned upon her, and decided that there was nothing for it but this marriage, which would make three of them unhappy for the rest of their lives—no, four; Mevrouw van Duyl didn't like Estelle either.

The morning passed quickly—too quickly, for Eliza enjoyed herself. The Professor was feeling quite himself again and was in a good mood, sitting cosily in a great armchair not too near the fire, arguing happily about the article they were writing, crossing out a great deal of the notes and filling in whole pages in his terrible spidery writing, and she, sitting at a table hastily set up in one corner of the room, typed what she was given. It was when they paused for coffee that he wanted to know what Estelle was doing.

'I hope she isn't annoyed with me, taking you away in this fashion,' he observed to Christian, looking quite unrepentant.

'She's gone out with Peters.' Christian's voice was casual. 'They share a consuming interest in Roman remains—I believe they intend to stay out for lunch.'

'But, my dear boy, you will see almost nothing of her. You go to your rooms tomorrow, don't you?'

'Yes—I've several patients lined up, I believe. Which reminds me to ask Eliza if she would like a lift into Nijmegen in the morning. I have to be back here after lunch, for I have a patient coming here to see me in the afternoon.'

'Of course she's dying to go,' said Professor Wyllie, giving her no chance to speak for herself. 'Besides, she must have off duty and all that.' He held out his cup for more coffee. 'I have letters to write and must have peace and quiet.'

Eliza handed him back his filled cup and said indignantly: 'Well, really, anyone would think I wore army boots and weighed half a ton! And you know quite well,' she went on, warming to her theme, 'that when you say you want to be quiet I hardly breathe.'

'All the more reason why you should go with Christian. You will be allowed to breathe—though to do you justice, girl, you are as light as a fairy on your feet, and twice as pretty.'

She didn't answer this piece of blatant flattery, but finished her coffee, and avoiding Christian's eye, went back to her typing.

They had finished the first draft by lunchtime and Eliza went downstairs to eat that meal with Mevrouw van Duyl and Doctor Berrevoets, who was leaving that afternoon, and of course, Christian. It was far nicer without Estelle, she considered, for everyone was light-hearted and talked a little nonsense, and Willy sat beside his master as he usually did. Afterwards she went back to her patient and coaxed him to lie down on his bed for a nap until tea time, when he was to get up and go downstairs for an hour or two. She was free now, she supposed; she was wondering what to do with her time when Nel came upstairs with a note from Mevrouw van Duyl, asking her if she would spend an hour with her in the small sitting room, so Eliza, glad of something to do, repaired downstairs. The room looked bright and welcoming, with its flickering fire and a lamp or two to brighten the gloom of the winter afternoon. She sat down a little shyly opposite her hostess.

'It was kind of you to ask me to come down,' she said.

'But, my dear, I have been wanting to do so, for I have had no chance to talk to you and I am full of curiosity. Perhaps you do not mind if today we talk like this, and later you shall be shown the house.' She nodded her small, silvery head. 'I wish to know about you,' she stated simply, a remark she instantly qualified by asking a string of questions about Eliza's work, her family and her likes and dislikes. Eliza answered her willingly enough—there was no point in doing otherwise; she had nothing to hide and the elder lady's interest was kindly. And presently she received her reward for her forbearance, for Mevrouw van Duyl embarked on a monologue about her son.

'He's thirty-seven,' she confided, 'and I have wished for years that he would marry, for I am not so young as

I was and there is a good deal to do here, and it seems that I am to have my wish.' She paused to sigh and Eliza felt sorry for her because her wish had turned sour on her. 'Christian works too hard,' she went on presently, 'for he has a great number of patients as well as work in the hospitals. He is very good at his work, you understand, my dear, and he loves it, just as he loves his home.' She sighed and Eliza said quickly: 'I suppose he's at his surgery this afternoon?'

'Oh, no, my dear. He went down to the village to see some of the old people there—those without families to help them, you know. He arranges for them to have help when that is the case and goes regularly to visit them. Willy has gone with him, and that means that they will go for a walk on the heath before they come home.'

'I love Willy—he must be a wonderful companion.'

'He is, we're excellent friends, he and I. Christian told me about Cat and how you found her—such a dear little creature and such pretty kittens. They will have a good home here, of that you may be sure. Christian will see to that.' She glanced at Eliza, who waited for her to go on, for it seemed as though she had more to say on the subject, but after a brief pause she went on to talk of other things and no more was said about her son. Eliza, listening to her hostess rambling on gently about this and that, thought what a dear little lady she was; Estelle couldn't know what a marvellous mother-in-law she was getting.

Half an hour later she got up to go, for the Professor would have to be wakened, tidied for his tea and shepherded downstairs. In the hall she met Estelle and Doctor Peters, returned from their outing. They were standing hand in hand and when they saw her, sprang guiltily apart, although to her eye they both seemed in high spirits; that was, as high-spirited as they were able to be. Eliza eyed them with some puzzlement—she quite liked Doctor Peters, although they had seldom had much to say to each other. He was what she described to herself as a worthy man and boring, but perhaps he and Estelle, both bores, didn't bore each other? It was an interesting point. She called a casual hullo to them as she went upstairs, then forgot about them because Professor Wyllie was ringing his bell.

She cast a professional eye over him, handed him his hairbrushes, found him a clean handkerchief and escorted him downstairs, where the rest of the party were assembled for their tea. Christian was there too, with Willy sitting very close to his master's chair. Eliza patted the noble animal's head as she slipped past to sit a little apart, happy to see the interest focused on Professor Wyllie, who, now that he felt almost well again, was showing the better side of his nature— indeed, he cornered the conversation, making Mevrouw van Duyl laugh a good deal. Everyone else laughed too, of course, but Eliza couldn't help noticing that Doctor Peters and Estelle were a little distrait, and Christian said almost nothing at all, although his eyes seldom left his fiancée's face.

She was on the point of uttering some polite excuse and slipping away to her room when Estelle suddenly suggested that they should go to the Rijn Hotel that evening. 'Such a lovely view of the river while we dine,' she pointed out with more animation than she had hitherto shown, 'and we can dance afterwards—besides, I have that new organza dress I'm longing to wear.'

She smiled round at everyone, sure that they would fall in with her wishes, and when her eyes lighted on Eliza, she added with exactly the right degree of politeness: 'And you too, of course, Eliza.'

Gathered into the general invitation with casual good manners, Eliza swallowed resentment and then stifled regret as she refused. There was nothing approximating to an evening dress amongst her few clothes hanging in the vast wall closet in her bedroom. She made polite excuses rather vaguely and went back to her room, saying that she had some typing to finish. She didn't see Christian again until several hours later, when she bumped into him in the long passage running from the conservatory to the front of the house. He looked splendid in his dinner jacket, but she didn't pause to take a better look, only murmured something or other and made to slip past him. Instead of which she found herself halted within an inch or so of his white shirt front, while a large hand clamped her shoulder fast.

'So—Eliza Proudfoot doesn't care to come out for the evening.' His voice was silky. 'Are we too frivolous for you, or is it that you don't care for our company?'

She studied the immaculate expanse of white before her eyes. 'Neither, Professor, it's just that I have the rest of the article to type, and besides that,' she hurried on, aware that he would dismiss that as a flimsy excuse, 'I have notes to write up and letters…if you don't mind, I should like to catch up on them. After all, I'm here to work.'

She took a cautious step backwards as she spoke and he stood on one side to let her pass with the casual courtesy which he might have accorded a stranger. Eliza made herself smile in his direction as she went past, and being an honest girl, spent the greater part of her lonely evening carefully typing what was left to be done, making out the charts Professor Wyllie had wanted and writing a number of quite unnecessary letters. And all the time she was doing this, a small, persistent portion of her mind was dwelling on the delights of the evening she was missing. But she couldn't have gone; she had glimpsed Estelle before they had all left, eye-catching in a lovely stained glass window dress which must have cost a small fortune. Even if she had had the pink skirt and the Marks and Spencer's top with her, she couldn't have completed with pure silk organza cut by an expert.

She told herself, once more, that the less she saw of Christian the better, quite forgetting that she was going to Nijmegen with him in the morning. Here, in this great house with its costly furnishing, he was different—no, not different, just unapproachable, someone who treated her with kindness and consideration but who was nevertheless dead set on marrying a wife who would be entirely suitable. Her fretful mind glossed over his strange whispered conversation of the previous evening, though she went on, talking out loud, because there was no fear of anyone hearing her. 'He's not in love with her at all, only she's the kind of wife he took it for granted he would marry.' She sighed, put away her writing case, and went to bed.

She prevailed on Professor Wyllie to remain in bed for his breakfast on the following morning, for although he was delighted with himself after his evening out, he was still tired. His pulse was up a little too; it would make a splendid excuse not to go with Christian, but in this she was forestalled by Professor Wyllie, who, when she mentioned the fact mildly, instantly commanded her to go, reminding her cunningly that he was far more likely to have a bad turn if he were crossed in his wishes. Eliza went down to her own breakfast torn between pleasure at the thought of spending some time with Christian, and a wish to carry out her resolution not to see so much of him. She was a little late for breakfast, loitering down the great staircase while she pondered about it.

Everyone was already seated at table; Mevrouw van Duyl, reading her post and drinking coffee, looked up to wish her a friendly good morning. Estelle was smoking a cigarette in a long holder and listening to a low-voiced monologue from Doctor Peters, and the master of the house sat at the head of the table, making inroads into his toast and marmalade and looking as black as thunder. He barely glanced at her as she sat down, and the atmosphere at his end of the table was so frosty that she made haste to drink some coffee, crumble a piece of toast and take herself off again.

Mevrouw waited until Eliza had left the room for some moments before remarking: 'Eliza looks tired.'

'Probably she got carried away with her typing and stayed up too late. She should have come with us,' ground out her son savagely.

Estelle put down her coffee cup with a little laugh. 'How ridiculously blind men can be,' she said with tolerant kindness. 'I daresay she did no work at all, poor little thing. How could she have come with us? She had no suitable clothes.'

He looked thunderstruck, then: 'Why didn't you lend her something of yours—heaven knows you've enough and to spare.'

She turned a mildly annoyed face to his. 'My dear Christian, lend her something of mine? You must be even more blind than I imagined. Eliza is small and just a little plump and, forgive me, not very distinguished. She would have looked ridiculous in any one of my gowns.'

She bridled smilingly under the dark eyes which raked her, ignoring his ferocious look. 'After all, she is the nurse, isn't she, not one of our guests. She would hardly bring evening clothes with her even if she had them. In any case, I don't suppose she knew anything about your way of life.'

There was no expression on his face when he answered her. 'No, Eliza had no idea of how I lived, but I must remind you that she is just as much a guest in my house as you are, Estelle. And in passing, I wasn't aware that you had invited her. I believe that inviting my friends to my home is still very much my own affair.' He got up from the table and went to kiss his mother. On the way to the door he said quite pleasantly:

'Let me put you right on something; I like small women, just a little plump, and with no urge to be distinguished.'

This remark had the effect of putting a satisfied gleam into his parent's eye, while Estelle, composed as always, turned to Doctor Peters and said in a low voice: 'He is so changed, I feel that I no longer need to consider him…'

Eliza was in Professor Wyllie's room, pottering around and wondering what she should do. Christian had said nothing about her going with him, and he had been in a nasty, cold temper; if she kept out of the way, he might go without her, and when they met later she could pretend that she had forgotten the whole arrangement. Better still, he might have forgotten about it too.

She was mistaken, for he came into the room at that very moment, wished his colleague a good morning and told her in a perfectly ordinary voice to get her coat and not keep him waiting. And something in his face caused her to obey him meekly without uttering a single word of dissent.

CHAPTER NINE

THE drive to Nijmegen was short and undertaken in silence. Eliza sat beside Christian in the Bentley convertible she had never seen before and which was still taking her breath at its subdued magnificence, and wondered what she was supposed to do. Would he put her down at some convenient spot in the city, and was she to make her own way back? Or would she be expected to meet him later? She was still mulling over these problems when they reached the city's outskirts, and by the time she had paused for a minute or two in her thinking to look around her, he had drawn up before a narrow house, one of a row, in a quiet, tree-lined street with a canal running down its centre. Presumably this was to be the convenient spot. She undid her safety belt and put a hand on the door handle, but not quickly enough, for he was out of his own seat and had opened her door while she was still trying to turn its handle. 'What time do you want me to be ready?' she asked in a bright little voice.

'Come inside and see my rooms,' he invited without answering her question. 'I'd like you to meet Ina, my secretary and right hand.'

Eliza felt an absurd jealousy of this paragon as they crossed the brick pavement and entered a narrow doorway. The house was used by several doctors, she saw, their names displayed on well-polished brass plates on the wall. Christian had the ground floor; he flung open a door and waved her into a pleasant room, empty save for a middle-aged woman in a white overall sitting at a desk under the window. She got up and smiled at them as they went in and spoke to him in Dutch, then when he introduced her to Eliza, switched over to English, her mild blue eyes studying her as she talked. She broke off in a few moments, however, to speak to Christian again, who answered her briefly, took Eliza by the arm and led her to a door at the back of the room. 'My first patient is due in ten minutes, just time to see the rest of the place.'

But in his consulting room he made no effort to show her anything, but stood looking out of the window at the quiet street below. 'I'll be ready by half past eleven,' he told her, 'then I have a hospital round to do—say an hour. Would you like to come with me? I'll get someone to show you round while I'm on the wards. I thought we might have lunch before we go back home.'

She was surprised and it showed in her face. 'Oh, how nice! I didn't expect…that is, I thought you would just pick me up when you'd finished.'

He smiled at her and she looked away quickly, because although she had steeled herself against his bad temper, she hadn't expected that he would look at her like that, disarming her completely.

'If you want to look round the shops—there are some rather nice ones—and come back here at about a quarter past eleven? So that we can all have coffee. You would like to have lunch with me, Eliza?'

She felt reckless under the dark-eyed, intent look. 'Yes, very much, thank you. Would you tell me the name of this street in case I miss my way?'

He wrote the address down and gave it to her. 'Have you enough money?' he asked her matter-of-factly.

'Yes, oh, yes, thanks. I don't want to buy a great deal—presents, that's all.'

He nodded and opened the door for her, and she crossed the waiting room which already held his first two patients, exchanging smiles with Ina as she went out.

She found the shopping streets easily enough and spent an hour buying cigars for her father, and for her mother a brooch, a garnet set in a gold circle, and then wandered round, to stare at the Town Hall and its statues and peer at the old houses with their quaint gables, but she didn't go far because she was afraid of being late for Christian. As it was she was exactly on time, and the three of them drank their coffee together in the waiting room. She spoke little because she could see that Christian had instructions and notes to give to Ina, who scrawled away in shorthand and yet had time to ask kindly of Eliza if she had enjoyed her tour of the shops. They left her to clear up presently, and went out to the car, and for want of anything else to talk about Eliza made the observation that the Bentley was quite super.

Christian had eased it into the thin stream of traffic. 'I'm glad you like her. She's a beauty to handle and much roomier than the Porsche 911s I sometimes use. My mother has a little car of her own—a small Mercedes—and she's a splendid driver, though I like Hub to be with her if I'm not there.' He turned into a narrow street, going slowly. 'My mother likes you.'

Eliza said readily: 'And I like your mother; she's kind and sweet,' and then, afraid that it sounded as though she had deliberately left Estelle out of it, she added: 'Estelle is very nice too.' Perhaps she had offended him, for he made no answer. It was a relief when he turned into a large paved courtyard and stopped outside the hospital entrance.

He was met at the door by two house doctors and a pretty girl in nurse's uniform whom he introduced as Lottie. 'She will take you round the place,' he explained. 'Be back here within the hour, will you?'

He was gone, striding along the corridor without a backward glance; Eliza suspected that he had already forgotten her. Lottie, though, seemed to know a good deal about her and her English was excellent. 'I am *Hoofd Zuster* of the Medical Floor,' she told Eliza, 'and

you are that also, are you not? We will therefore go first
to that part of the hospital.'

She led the way down the same corridor as Christian
had taken and the pair of them wandered happily in and
out of small, modern wards, each patient with his or her
own intercom and a nurses' station in each broad
corridor. It was all well planned, light and airy, and the
nurses looked exactly like the nurses in Eliza's own
hospital, and when she remarked on this, they had an
interesting exchange of views about caps and uniforms
and whether it was best to live in or out. They became
so engrossed that they had to hurry through the Surgical
Wing, the Children's Unit and the Theatre Block, where
they paused again to compare notes on the Intensive
Care Unit, and only a glance at the clock prevented them
from continuing this absorbing chat and caused them to
hurry back to the entrance, to arrive just as Christian
appeared in the corridor. Lottie went over to him and
spoke laughingly, then said in English: 'We have had so
much to talk about, you must please allow Eliza to come
again, for there is a great deal she has yet to see.'

He looked interested. 'I'll see that she does,' he
promised without saying how that would be arranged,
so that Eliza guessed that he was just being polite, for
as far as she could see, she would only be in Holland
for a few more days. Professor Wyllie had finished his
article and even allowing for a day or two's holiday, he
must surely be thinking of returning soon. She got back

into the car and when he was beside her thanked him for arranging the visit. 'Lottie was so sweet,' she told him, 'and I really enjoyed it.'

He started the car. 'Yes, she's very popular and the senior Sister on the Medical side. You liked the hospital?'

There was plenty to talk about as he drove through the city and out on to the motorway towards Arnhem, but presently Eliza broke off in mid-sentence to say: 'We didn't come this way this morning.'

'No. We're going to a place on the Rhine for lunch. The view is charming and I've booked a window table so that we can watch the barges going up and down the river.' He turned to smile at her. 'We'll go home on one of the quieter roads and cross the river at Ochten instead of going through Nijmegen again.'

The hotel was rather splendid and its restaurant even more so. Eliza was glad that she wearing the good tweed coat and had put on the prettier of her two dresses, a pleasing garment of green and brown which matched her eyes. She saw Christian's look of approval as they sat down, and glowed under it. But he said nothing, only called her attention to the promised view and asked her what she would like to drink. She chose Dubonnet and then, under his guidance, decided on *Croquettes de Turbot Sauce Homard* followed by a *Soufflé aux Pêches*. She wasn't quite sure what this might be—a pancake with peaches didn't seem quite exquisite enough for their surroundings, but the turbot was delicious, washed down with a Chablis which her companion assured her would make the meal all the more enjoyable. He was quite right; by the time the dessert arrived, she was feeling very much at ease with him. It was like being back at Inverpolly; they had quarrelled often enough while they were there, but there had been times when they had been good friends, just as they were now. She beamed across the table at him. 'This is quite super, you know. What a lot I shall have to tell everyone when I get back!'

She eyed the confection on her plate and saw that it was very worthy of its opulent surroundings—peaches, Kirsch, apricot sauce and piles of whipped cream. She ate it with pleasure and no self-conscious remarks about putting on weight, while Christian ate his cheese and biscuits and watched her with a gleam in his eyes which she failed to see. They drank their coffee, still talking with the enthusiasm of two people who have discovered each other for the first time and then, quite reluctantly, went back to the car.

Perhaps it was the Chablis which emboldened her to ask: 'Why were you so cross yesterday when I said I wouldn't go out to dinner?'

'I thought, mistakenly, that you didn't want to come.'

'Who told you that I did?' she wanted to know suspiciously.

'Estelle—at least, she felt sure that you did and refused because you had no dress to wear, although she didn't say this until breakfast this morning.'

'She said that?' Eliza's voice was a little shrill with indignation. 'Well…' words failed her. After a few minutes she said: 'She was quite right, actually.'

He said gravely: 'Yes, I supposed she was, but I'm ashamed that I didn't think of it at the time; I was only ready to believe that you merely wished to vex me.'

They were going quite slowly along a country road, well away from Nijmegen. Eliza looked at the quiet fields sliding past, wondering how to answer that, and said finally: 'No, I had no wish to do that, it's just that I do vex you sometimes, don't I, without meaning to—or most of the time anyway.' She missed his little smile as she went on: 'Thank you for my outing, it was kind of you.'

'My pleasure. Besides, I wanted to take you to that particular restaurant, for it's as pleasant by day as it is in the evening.'

Enlightenment was painful. 'That's where you all went last night?' She didn't wait for him to answer, because she was sure that it was so. 'You took me there because of what Estelle said.' Her voice trembled with outraged pride. 'She didn't ask you to take me?'

'Of course not.' His surprise was comfortingly genuine.

'You invited me out of pity…' She stammered a little, her pretty face quite pink.

He drew into the side of the road and switched off the engine and turned to face her. 'No. If you remember I asked you to come with me to Nijmegen yesterday

morning and I had already formed the intention of
taking you out to lunch. Why are you so annoyed?'

It was difficult to put into words; in the end she gave
up and said in a rather mumbling voice: 'I'm not.' There
was really nothing she could add, she decided, and added
with the air of someone making polite conversation:

'When is Professor Wyllie going home?'

If he found the change of conversation a little unexpected he gave no sign. 'The day after tomorrow, I believe.'

So that, thought Eliza, was that. She had achieved
nothing; Christian would marry Estelle and be unhappy
ever after, which was very silly, because it was evident
to any female eye that Estelle rather liked Doctor Peters,
who definitely liked her… What a stupid situation,
when all it needed was one person to speak the truth.
And now it was too late. She bit her lip with vexation,
knowing that her hands were tied and even if she had
succeeded in charming him away from Estelle there
would always be the vexed question as to whether she
had wanted him for his money. Perhaps it was better like
this. She said overbrightly: 'Don't you have to get back
for your patient?'

He had been watching her while she thought; now he
laughed softly as he started the car, and she wondered
why. She made stilted conversation for the rest of the
short journey and once indoors, flew upstairs with a
murmured excuse that she had things to do. She heard
him chuckling to himself as she reached the landing.

She didn't see him again until dinner time, and then everyone else was there too. She had already told Professor Wyllie about her outing; Mevrouw van Duyl was the only other person who wanted to know if she had enjoyed herself; Estelle and Doctor Peters were too engrossed in planning another trip to more Roman remains to do more than wish her a civil good evening, and Christian, when he joined them, was a charming host and that was all. What he was really thinking behind that bland face was anyone's guess.

Eliza tackled Professor Wyllie about their return before he went to bed that night; she had made one or two efforts to speak to him in the drawing room after dinner and had been frustrated; the old man had gone off with Christian after half an hour or so and not returned until almost eleven o'clock, leaving her to keep Mevrouw van Duyl company while the other two continued making their plans for the next day. Eliza waited until her patient had made his good nights, then did the same and followed him upstairs.

'Professor van Duyl tells me that you are going back to England the day after tomorrow,' she began without beating about the bush. 'You didn't say anything to me, though. When exactly do you want to leave, because I'll need to take a look at the car. Are we going back the way we came?'

He mumbled something about not being sure and then observed testily that he wasn't in the mood to be plagued with a lot of planning at that hour of night. 'Time enough tomorrow,' he told her, and sent her off to bed.

Eliza wakened early, and unable to sleep again got up and looked out of the window. It was early February now and still winter, yet the garden carried a hint of spring in the morning half-light from a clear sky which promised sunshine later. And as she looked, Christian came round the house, striding across the lawn, Willy beside him. Presently, she knew, he would be going to his surgery and the hospital, and she thought wistfully that it would have been nice to have gone with him again. If Professor Wyllie chose to leave early the following morning, she wouldn't see much more of Christian. It was a saddening thought, but she threw it off, got dressed and finding Professor Wyllie asleep, went downstairs to find Hub, who willingly enough allowed her to visit Cat, who had just enjoyed a good breakfast and was lying back while the kittens enjoyed theirs. The little beast blinked at her and purred, looking the picture of content, and Eliza said: 'She's sweet, isn't she, Hub? I suppose Willy has gone with his master?'

'Yes, miss, half an hour ago. Would you like your breakfast now?'

She breakfasted alone, for it was still early, wondering as she ate at what hour the servants got up; the whole place shone and sparkled already and there was a cheerful coming and going of people, half of whom she hadn't yet seen. It was fantastic, in this day and age, to come across a house so well run and so well staffed.

She was on her way upstairs again when she remembered something and ran down again to ask Hub, in the hall sorting the post: 'Does Professor van Duyl really own the Lodge at Inverpolly?'

He had acquired his master's calm way of never looking surprised. 'Yes, miss. He hasn't been there very often in the last few years, though, but only yesterday he was telling me that the place is to be decorated and refurbished.'

She longed to ask more questions, but didn't like to. Christian had told her that Estelle didn't like the Scottish Highlands, or had she changed her mind since his return? It seemed unlikely. Eliza recalled the lonely place with something like homesickness as she went slowly up the staircase again.

She spent a wretched morning, typing notes from Professor Wyllie's spidery hand, for as he explained to her, there would probably be a second article in the course of time and Christian might as well be given some of the data he might require before they left. But she was finished by lunchtime and went downstairs to find Mevrouw van Duyl and Professor Wyllie drinking sherry together.

'Estelle and Doctor Peters are out,' explained her hostess in a dry voice. 'Probably they have decided to return later in the day.' She looked at Eliza with bright-eyed intentness. 'Go and take that uniform off, child, and then come and have lunch; I'm sure you don't need to be a nurse any longer. Why not go for a walk this afternoon? Just in the park, perhaps? There is a charming lake beyond the trees.'

Eliza went and put on the grey dress and did her hair very tidily, so that only a very few curls escaped the pins. The sherry she had had lent a sparkle to her eyes and the two elderly people waiting for her smiled indulgently at her as she joined them. The three of them had an enjoyable meal together, and presently, when they had had their coffee, she left them sitting by the fire in the small sitting room and went to fetch her coat.

It was cold outside but pleasant in the thin sunshine. Eliza buried her chin in the folds of her head-scarf, stuck her gloved hands into her coat pockets and started off briskly, down the formal garden, through the door in the wall, and into the park beyond. She cut across the grass here towards the group of trees which concealed the pond, and had just reached the first of them and glimpsed the water when she heard voices. Estelle and Doctor Peters, standing very close together and only a few yards from her—and Estelle was speaking in a high, clear voice which penetrated the thicket with remarkable clarity, what was more, she was speaking in English. 'It was a great mistake in the first place,' she was assuring her companion. 'I see now that we are not compatible, he and I…' She turned her head as Eliza trod on a twig. 'Why are you standing there?' she asked coldly.

'Because I came out for a walk, and how can I help

but hear you when you choose to talk like a tragedy queen?' asked Eliza snappishly. 'And I'm glad to hear that you've realised at last that you and Christian don't suit—I hope you'll have the sense to break it off and leave him free to make his own plans…'

Estelle had taken a step towards her, but now she stopped abruptly, her blue eyes wide.

'So kind,' said Christian to the back of Eliza's head, 'of you to allow me to arrange my own future, although I have my doubts about it.'

He walked past her petrified form to where Estelle was standing, remembering to nod to Doctor Peters. 'I came looking for you,' he told her blandly. 'I thought it was time that we had a talk.' His eyes rested for a moment on Doctor Peters. 'But it seems that most of my talking has been done for me.' He held out a hand. 'I take it that we are no longer to be married—but friends just the same, I hope.'

Estelle's face took on a slightly frustrated look; she wasn't being allowed to squeeze a single dramatic moment from the scene, although she made the most of removing the ring from her finger, forestalled however by Christian's cheerful: 'No, no—keep it, do. I never liked it, you know. You shall have the earrings for a wedding present.' He turned away, leaving her breathing heavily with annoyance, caught Eliza by the arm and dragged her along with him.

'Musn't stay there,' he told her briskly. 'Leave them

in peace to discuss their Roman remains—there's nothing they like better.'

He didn't speak again and Eliza hurried along beside him, still held firmly by the elbow so that even if she could have thought of something to say, she wouldn't have had the breath to spare. They gained the side door at last and she muttered: 'I'm going upstairs...'

'No, you're not,' his voice was mild but decisive. He turned down another passage and opened the door into the covered verandah which ran along the back of the house. It was almost warm here in the winter sunshine. Eliza, freed at last of his compelling hand, went and stood at its wrought iron railing, looking down on to the small garden below, where early daffodils were beginning to show amongst the crocus and the grape hyacinths. In the distance she could see Estelle and Doctor Peters, still a long way away, emerging from the trees.

'So you decided that Estelle wasn't suitable for me and set about putting an end to our engagement, Eliza?' Christian's voice was bland, the voice he used when he didn't want anyone to know what his real feelings were.

She said: 'I don't know how you knew that. Yes,' without looking round.

'And may I ask if you intend to interfere with any future plans I may have—marriage-wise?'

She shook her head. 'No. I was going to, you know. You see I knew that Estelle wasn't the right wife for you and I knew you didn't love her; it would never have done

at all. I-I meant to marry you myself.' She swallowed
back tears at the mere thought and went on in a matter-
of-fact way: 'But that was before I knew that you had
all this—I thought you were just a doctor.'

'I am just a doctor, Eliza.'

'Oh, no, you're not. You—we don't belong to the
same world and it's no good saying different. My mother
and father—I'm proud of them, but they're not…'

'I found them delightful.'

She whirled round to face him, forgetful of the tears
on her cheeks. 'When? How did you find…?'

'I went to visit them. You see, when I got back home
I realised that Estelle and I—I went down to meet your
parents, Eliza, and I liked them immensely and I hope
they liked me.'

'It doesn't make any difference.' She had turned her
back on him again, remembering the tears. 'This house
and the park—why, I've never seen so many people
about the place—just to look after you.'

'Regrettable, perhaps, but they depend on me, you
see, just as they depended on my father and his father
before him.' He smiled a little at the back of her head.
'I pay them,' he pointed out mildly. 'Besides, when I
marry they will have my wife to look after and in the
course of time, a bunch of high-spirited children.'

She found herself asking: 'High-spirited? How do
you know that?'

'I have always considered you to be that, my darling;

children normally have some, at least, of the character-istics of their mother.' He smiled again. 'Tell me, how did you know that I didn't love Estelle?'

He had called her his darling, or had she dreamt it? 'You kissed me—that day the cottage was flooded. I don't think that a man who loved a girl enough to want to marry her would kiss another girl in that fashion.' She wiped her tears away with one hand. 'Oh, dear, and I made you sweep the floor.'

'An experience I thoroughly enjoyed. We must make sure that our sons learn the rudiments of house cleaning.'

Eliza said in a choking voice: 'Oh, please—I've been very silly, but at least I've been honest about it, only please don't make a joke of it.'

'Turn around, Eliza, and look at me.' He was leaning against the verandah wall, his hands in his pockets. 'Am I joking?' he asked gently, and when she looked at him she could see that he wasn't, so that her mouth curved in a smile. 'I'm most unsuitable,' she told him, 'I…'

She was given no chance to say any more; he had left the wall and his arms were holding her close. 'I see no alternative,' he told her softly, 'and I find you most suitable. Indeed, I cannot imagine my life without you, my little love.'

He bent to kiss her, and presently, when she had her breath again, she observed into his shoulder: 'I find it very strange, for you didn't like me at first, did you?'

'Now what gave you that idea? I liked you all too

much; I found Estelle dwindling away to a cardboard figure which had nothing to do with me and I knew then that she never had, though I tried very hard to believe that that was not so. But you drew me like a magnet—it was as though I had my feet on a path which led to you and no one and nothing else. "When a man finds his way, Heaven is gentle"—someone wrote that, I don't know who, but it's true; I found my way just in time, didn't I, dear heart?'

He kissed her again, taking his time, and Eliza stirred in his arms and said, half laughing: 'Oh, Christian, they can see us.'

Estelle and Doctor Peters had come into the garden below them, but Christian took no notice of her, but kissed her once more. Only then did he remark: 'Good, perhaps it will encourage them to do the same. They shall come to our wedding—it might put the idea of their marrying each other into their heads.'

'I'm still waiting to be asked,' she reminded him a little tartly.

'Ah, yes, I was coming to that, my darling. Come into the study. There will be no one—only Cat and Willy and the kittens—to disturb us there, and I will ask you to marry me in a manner which you will never forget as long as you live.'

She reached up to kiss him. 'That sounds very satisfactory. I'll come and hear what you have to say,' said Eliza.

Turn the page for a sneak preview
of the first book in the new miniseries
DIAMONDS DOWN UNDER
from Silhouette Desire®,
VOWS & A VENGEFUL GROOM
by Bronwyn Jameson

Available January 2008

Silhouette Desire®
Always Powerful, Passionate and Provocative

Kimberley Blackstone didn't notice the waiting horde of media until it was too late. Flashbulbs exploded around her like a New Year's light show. She skidded to a halt, so abruptly her trailing suitcase all but overtook her.

This had to be a case of mistaken identity. Surely. Kimberley hadn't been on the paparazzi hit list for close to a decade, not since she'd estranged herself from her billionaire father and his headline-hungry diamond business.

But no, it was *her* name they called. *Her* face was the focus of a swarm of lenses that circled her like avid hornets. Her heart started to pound with fear-fueled adrenaline.

What did they want?

What was going on?

With a rising sense of bewilderment she scanned the crowd for a clue, and her gaze fastened on a tall, leonine figure forcing his way to the front. A tall, familiar figure. Her head came up in stunned recognition, and their gazes collided across the sea of heads before the cameras erupted with another barrage of flashes, this time right in her exposed face.

Blinded by the flashbulbs—and by the shock of that momentary eye-meet—Kimberley didn't realize his intent until he'd forged his way to her side, possibly by the sheer strength of his personality. She felt his arm wrap around her shoulder, pulling her into the protective shelter of his body, allowing her no time to object. No chance to lift her hands to ward him off.

In the space of a hastily drawn breath, she found herself plastered knee-to-nose against six feet two inches of hard-bodied male.

Ric Perrini.

Her lover for ten torrid weeks, her husband for ten tumultuous days.

Her ex for ten tranquil years.

After all this time, he should not have felt so familiar but, oh dear, he did. She knew the scent of that body and its lean, muscular strength. She knew its heat and its slick power and every response it could draw from hers.

She also recognized the ease with which he'd taken control of the moment and the decisiveness of his deep voice when it rumbled close to her ear. "I have a car waiting outside. Is this your only luggage?"

Kimberley nodded. "I assume you will tell me," she said tightly, "what this welcome party is all about."

"Not while the welcome party is within earshot. No."

Barking a request for the cameramen to stand aside, Perrini took her hand and pulled her into step with his ground-eating stride. Kimberley let him, because he was right, damn his arrogant, Italian-suited hide. Despite the speed with which he whisked her across the airport terminal, she could almost feel the hot breath of the pursuing media on her back.

This was neither the time nor the place for explanations. Inside his car, however, she would get answers.

Now that the initial shock had been blown away—by the haste of their retreat, by the heat of her gathering indignation, by the rush of adrenaline fired by Perrini's presence and the looming verbal battle—her brain was starting to tick over. This had to be her father's doing. And if it was a Howard Blackstone publicity ploy, then it had to be about Blackstone Diamonds, the company that ruled his life.

The knowledge made her chest tighten with a familiar ache of disillusionment.

She'd known her father would be flying in from Sydney for today's opening of the newest in his chain of exclusive, high-end jewelry boutiques. The opulent shopfront sat adjacent to the rival business where Kimberley worked. No coincidence, she thought bitterly, just as it was no coincidence that Ric Perrini was here in Auckland ushering her to his car.

Perrini was Howard Blackstone's right-hand man,

second in command at Blackstone Diamonds, a legacy of his short-lived marriage to the boss's daughter. No doubt her father had sent him to fetch her; the question was *why?*

* * * * *

Get swept away down under with the glitz and glamour of the Blackstone empire as Kimberley tries to determine the real reason behind her "reunion" with Ric….

Look for VOWS & A VENGEFUL GROOM
by Bronwyn Jameson,
in stores January 2008.

When Kimberley Blackstone's father is
presumed dead, Kimberley is required to take
over the helm of Blackstone Diamonds. She
has to work closely with her ex, Ric Perrini, to
battle not only the press, but also the fierce
attraction still sizzling between them. Does Ric
feel the same...or is it the power her share of
Blackstone Diamonds will provide him as he
battles for boardroom supremacy.

Look for

VOWS &
A VENGEFUL GROOM

by

BRONWYN
JAMESON

Available January wherever you buy books

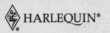

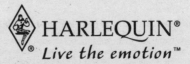

REQUEST YOUR FREE BOOKS!
2 FREE NOVELS PLUS 2
FREE GIFTS!

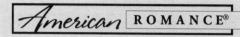

Heart, Home & Happiness!

YES! Please send me 2 FREE Harlequin American Romance® novels and my 2 FREE gifts. After receiving them, if I don't wish to receive any more books, I can return the shipping statement marked "cancel." If I don't cancel, I will receive 4 brand-new novels every month and be billed just $4.24 per book in the U.S., or $4.99 per book in Canada, plus 25¢ shipping and handling per book and applicable taxes, if any*. That's a savings of close to 15% off the cover price! I understand that accepting the 2 free books and gifts places me under no obligation to buy anything. I can always return a shipment and cancel at any time. Even if I never buy another book from Harlequin, the two free books and gifts are mine to keep forever.

154 HDN EEZK   354 HDN EEZV

Name _____ (PLEASE PRINT) _____

Address _____ Apt. # _____

City _____ State/Prov. _____ Zip/Postal Code _____

Signature (if under 18, a parent or guardian must sign)

Mail to the **Harlequin Reader Service®**:
IN U.S.A.: P.O. Box 1867, Buffalo, NY 14240-1867
IN CANADA: P.O. Box 609, Fort Erie, Ontario L2A 5X3

Not valid to current Harlequin American Romance subscribers.

Want to try two free books from another line?
Call 1-800-873-8635 or visit www.morefreebooks.com.

* Terms and prices subject to change without notice. NY residents add applicable sales tax. Canadian residents will be charged applicable provincial taxes and GST. This offer is limited to one order per household. All orders subject to approval. Credit or debit balances in a customer's account(s) may be offset by any other outstanding balance owed by or to the customer. Please allow 4 to 6 weeks for delivery.

Your Privacy: Harlequin is committed to protecting your privacy. Our Privacy Policy is available online at www.eHarlequin.com or upon request from the Reader Service. From time to time we make our lists of customers available to reputable firms who may have a product or service of interest to you. If you would prefer we not share your name and address, please check here. ☐

HAR07

Inside ROMANCE

Stay up-to-date on all your romance reading news!

Inside Romance is a FREE quarterly newsletter highlighting our upcoming series releases and promotions.

Visit

www.eHarlequin.com/InsideRomance

to sign up to receive our complimentary newsletter today!

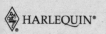

Every great love has a story to tell™

Nick and Stefanie Marsden met in
high school, fell in love and married
four years later. But thirty years later,
when Nick goes missing, everything—
love and life itself—hangs in the balance
during this long winter night. A night of
memories. A night of hope and faith…

Look for

The Vow

by

Rebecca Winters

Available January wherever you buy books.

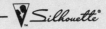